Party On

This is it, Preston thought. *This is the moment!*

He pressed between the other partygoers, making his way to the table. He vaguely heard Woody behind him, going on and on about his favorite moments during their school years together, but Preston paid him no attention. He was too busy taking a few deep breaths, steeling himself for his fateful encounter with Amanda Beckett.

"Am . . ." It was all he could manage.

She looked at *him!* Amanda looked directly into his eyes!

"Am—"

"And how about that time when we went on the field trip to the meat-packing plant and you threw up in you bookbag?" Woody came to Preston's side. "That was the *funniest!*"

Preston looked at Woody.

Amanda looked at Woody.

Mortified, Preston turned to Amanda. She was looking him again. She looked . . . *embarrassed* for him. She averted her eyes, then turned and walked away from the table.

Preston's heart d~~ropped~~

The party was o

CAN'T HARDLY WAIT

A novelization by **Ray Garton**
Based on the screenplay written by
Deborah Kaplan & **Harry Elfont**

POCKET BOOKS
New York   London   Toronto   Sydney   Tokyo   Singapore

This book is a work of fiction. Names, characters, places and incidents are products of the author's imagination or are used fictitiously. Any resemblance to actual events or locales or persons, living or dead, is entirely coincidental.

An *Original* Publication of POCKET BOOKS

POCKET BOOKS, a division of Simon & Schuster Inc.
1230 Avenue of the Americas, New York, NY 10020

Copyright © 1998 by Columbia Pictures Industries, Inc. All Rights Reserved.

Motion Picture Artwork and Photography copyright © 1998 by Columbia Pictures Industries, Inc. All Rights Reserved.

ISBN: 0-671-02645-3

First Pocket Books printing June 1998

10 9 8 7 6 5 4 3 2 1

POCKET and colophon are registered trademarks of Simon & Schuster Inc.

Printed in the U.S.A.

This book is for
Dawn
With Love

Acknowledgments

My thanks to Deborah Kaplan and Harry Elfont for writing such a fun script, and to my agent, Ricia Mainhardt, my editor, Lisa Clancy, and her assistant, Liz Shiflett, three of the finest people in the publishing business.

CAN'T HARDLY WAIT

Chapter 1

"**Y**OU'RE NOT GONNA *BELIEVE* WHAT HAPPENED!"

Preston Myers cut into the line of graduates waiting to turn in their caps and gowns. "Denise?" He grabbed the arm of his best friend, Denise Fleming.

"This is such a load of bull," she said. She was reading her diploma, the graduation gown draped over her arm and dragging on the ground.

"Um, excuse me, but did you *hear* me just now?" Preston asked.

"*Hah!*" she blurted. "Listen to this: 'Huntington High is proud to confer. . . .' *Please,* like they even know who I am!"

Preston and Denise were old friends. They'd gone to school together since first grade, then had dated briefly in the eighth grade, but without success. They'd found that they made great friends, though,

1

and had remained close ever since their early, short-lived romance.

They had just graduated from Huntington High School that morning. As soon as Preston and Denise turned in their caps and gowns they were free. And, tonight they would be going to the big graduation party at Molly Stinson's house.

Preston took the paper from Denise and rolled it back up. "I just talked to Matt Wachinski. He said that Mike Dexter just broke up with Amanda Beckett! Here, at graduation! Can you believe it?"

"Oh, the Amanda thing," Denise said, nodding. "I heard that earlier. Kira Mitchell told me before the pictures."

"And you didn't tell *me?*" he asked, shocked. "How could you not *tell* me?"

"Because I knew you'd react like this."

"Well, how am I *supposed* to react?" Preston asked, ignoring the other kids yelling and pushing past him. "Amanda Beckett's not *supposed* to be single!" He moved forward in line.

"Oh, God, Pres," Denise said, following him. "You really should move on, you know."

"I *have!*" He cut the line and headed for the nearest table. He dropped his cap and gown in front of the coach, who crossed his name off a list. "Meyers!" She boomed. "Check."

Preston turned to Denise. "This morning, I told myself that very thing. Move on. Amanda and Mike are still together, they're *never* gonna break up, I should go on to college, meet someone who's right for me, forget all about Amanda until I see her at our

2

reunion and she's all fat and Mike's bald and paunchy."

Denise chuckled and smiled. "Now *that* would be justice."

"I *know!* And then I'd tell my wife, 'See that fat woman over there? I was madly in love with her in high school.' And my wife would say, *'That* one? *Really?'* And we'd have a good laugh about it, and that would be it. The end. It's over."

"Sounds great," Denise said with a shrug. "So what's the problem?"

Preston twirled his class tassel while Denise fumbled to remove hers from her cap.

"Get a move on, Fleming!" the coach barked.

"The problem is, that's not what *happened*," he went on. "Don't you see? This party tonight, Amanda's suddenly single . . . everything's falling into place!"

Denise rolled her eyes. "Pres, it's just a coincidence."

"No, no," he said, taking her gown from her arm and brushing the dirt from the football field off the hem. "I don't believe in coincidences. The planets have realigned and they're, like . . . waving me home! Don't you see? It's fate. *Fate* has given me a window."

"A mighty small window, considering you're leaving for Boston tomorrow."

Preston hesitated. "Oh, yeah. Well, uh . . ."

" 'Well, uh' *what?"* Denise asked, eyes widening. "All you've been talking about this whole year is how you would give *anything* to go to this summer

3

writing workshop with Kurt Vonnegut! You're gonna blow off Kurt Vonnegut for *Amanda*? Where are your *priorities?*" She pushed her cap toward the coach and dragged Preston back toward the field, where parents and friends still roamed about, shooting photos. "C'mon, Preston . . . it's Kurt *Vonnegut*. I mean, *look* at him. He's pretty old, he could *die* soon!"

"Don't say that," Preston said, wincing. He stopped at the last row of chairs set up on the field and looked up at the goalposts, now toilet-papered. "I'm *not* gonna blow it off."

"What happened to Amanda getting fat?" Denise asked with a smirk.

"Nah, she doesn't strike me as the type to get fat."

"Oh, you'd be surprised who gets fat and who doesn't. Ever seen Elizabeth Taylor in *National Velvet?*"

Preston chuckled as he went through the rows, looking under chairs for his backpack.

"Whatever," Denise said, shaking her head. "Like it's even gonna happen. You've never even had a *conversation* with her. In four whole years, you've—"

"It's not about conversations," Preston insisted. "It's about a *connection*. Amanda and I are connected somehow. We have been ever since the first day she came to school . . ."

Denise slumped in a chair, kicking aside discarded programs, and buried her face in her hands. "Oh, no, please don't tell me about it. Not *again.*"

Preston ignored her. "October, freshman year. It was the first time in history I ever missed the bus . . ."

On that fateful October day of his freshman year, Preston was dropped off by his dad in the school parking lot. At the very moment that Preston got out of his dad's car, a beautiful, mesmerizing girl got out of another car just a few yards away. Preston watched the girl walk toward the school, hypnotized by her beauty.

Had he caught the bus that morning and arrived at school on time, Preston knew he would have missed her. Instead, he was the first person at Huntington High to lay eyes on Amanda Beckett, the school's newest student.

To Preston, it seemed like fate.

Before he'd missed the bus that morning, Preston had missed breakfast. As he sat in his first class of the day, he removed from his bookbag the strawberry Pop-Tart his mother had given him on his way out the door. It was then . . . at that very moment . . . that Amanda walked into the classroom.

Every student turned to watch her walk up to the front of the class and talk quietly with the teacher, Mrs. Graves. After a moment, Mrs. Graves introduced Amanda to the class, then assigned her a seat—right next to Preston.

Preston took a deep breath and closed his eyes for a moment.

Okay, he thought. *She gets out of her car the same*

time I get out of mine . . . walks into the same class I'm in . . . gets seated right next to me . . . but it's just coincidence, that's all. Just coincidence.

He calmed the fluttering in his stomach, opened his eyes, and forced himself not to turn and stare at the beautiful girl sitting at the desk next to him. He took another bite of the strawberry Pop-Tart and chewed slowly. It wasn't long before he gave in and turned casually to glance at Amanda. He didn't glance, though; he *gawked*.

Amanda was eating a Pop-Tart, too. A *strawberry* Pop-Tart! Preston's absolute *favorite* Pop-Tart flavor! One of his favorite foods in the whole *world!*

Preston stared at Amanda in awe . . . then at her Pop-Tart in awe . . . then at *his* Pop-Tart in awe. Preston knew that *this* was no coincidence, and that meant that *none* of it had been coincidence. It was obvious to him that he and Amanda Beckett were being drawn together by some higher power, some greater force, something bigger than both of them, bigger than *all* of them. But Preston had no idea how to react to what was so obviously the intervening hand of fate. He wondered what he should do next, how he should proceed. And as he was wondering, fate intervened again.

"Who would like to volunteer to give Amanda a tour of the school?" Mrs. Graves asked.

A smile grew slowly on Preston's face. A tour of the school . . . it would be the *perfect* opportunity for him to get to know the girl whom the stars had clearly chosen as his soul mate. He would show her around the school . . . and at the same time, maybe

6

she would realize what he already knew . . . that they were *meant* for each other.

Preston started to raise his hand to get Mrs. Graves's attention . . . but he hesitated. Would a girl that beautiful want to be led all over campus by . . . *him?* By a . . . *nobody?*

A second later, Preston rejected that thought and started to raise his hand again and opened his mouth to say—

"I will," Mike Dexter said, walking up the aisle. He stopped at Amanda's desk and smiled down at her.

Amanda rose, smiling at him. Seconds later, the two of them were gone.

"That's where I lost her," Preston said to Denise, returning with his backpack, a Kurt Vonnegut novel sticking out of one pocket. "I had a clear shot and I hesitated. But fate's finally given me a second chance."

Denise let out a long sigh. "Fate . . . Pop-Tarts . . . and all of this makes *sense* to you? Were you dropped on your soft spot as an infant, Pres? What is *wrong* with you?"

Preston chuckled. "What's wrong with *me?* What the hell's wrong with Mike *Dexter?*" He turned to her and smiled. "Well, I'm ready to go if you are. How do I look?" He wore a short-sleeved blue shirt open in front over a white T-shirt with orange trim.

"You look fine," Denise said, straightening her large glasses. "How about me?"

She wore a vintage black leather jacket, knee-length and wraparound, that she'd bought at a secondhand store where she did a good deal of her shopping. Beneath it, she wore a gray crocheted sweater and black jeans.

"You look a little like Dracula," Preston said, smiling. "You really need to add some color to your wardrobe."

"Color? You mean, as in your colorful imagination? Fate . . . Pop-Tarts . . . the planets realigning." She punched him on the shoulder and said, "C'mon, let's go."

They walked to the edge of the field, skirting some families taking photos in the end zone.

Preston's beat-up old Cadillac was parked behind the bleachers. Once they were inside, Preston started the engine. "You know," he said, turning to Denise with a smile, "I can't believe he actually broke up with her."

Chapter 2

"I CAN'T BELIEVE YOU ACTUALLY BROKE UP WITH HER, Mike," Jake Wickley said as he chewed on a mouthful of fries.

While Preston was shaking his head, Mike Dexter was at Big Burger with his three best friends, Jake, who sat next to him, and Ben Foss and T. J. Munson, who sat across the table. They were all wearing black jeans and tight T-shirts, eating Extra-Big Burgers with fries and drinking beers from the six-pack they'd sneaked in. They talked as they ate. Mouths full.

Mike washed down a large bite of his burger with a gulp of beer, then leaned back and scratched his chest. "Well, it's like I always say, guys . . ." He opened his mouth and released a long, loud, wet belch.

9

All four of them broke into laughter at that.

"But Amanda was so hot, man," Ben said after they'd calmed down.

T.J.'s head bobbed up and down rapidly in agreement. *"So* hot," he said enthusiastically, spraying some sesame seeds from his full mouth.

Mike had been hearing the same thing from guys all day, ever since he'd broken up with Amanda that morning at graduation. He and Amanda had been dating for four years. They'd been four great years, too. It made him feel pretty good to be the steady boyfriend of the most beautiful, sought-after girl at school. He'd always considered himself to be pretty cool, but *that* made him even cooler.

But breaking up with Amanda was something else altogether. Mike had wondered how people would react once word got around. Everyone had been shocked by the news. No one could believe he'd actually *done* it. It took a special *kind* of cool to break up with the most beautiful, sought-after girl at school. The reactions he'd been getting all day made Mike realize that breaking up with Amanda had elevated him to a whole new level of cool, one that he'd been unable to achieve by simply *dating* Amanda. It felt good. It felt *great*.

"Yeah, she was hot, I guess," Mike said, picking up his Extra-Big Burger. "For a *high school* girl." He looked at the guys across the table from him, waiting for a reaction.

Jake and Ben and T.J. stopped chewing and stared at him blankly.

"Come *on*, guys," Mike went on. "We're not in

high school anymore, okay? Well, uh"—he shrugged and wrinkled his nose in disgust—"except for those bogus remedial classes, I mean. Look, we're gonna be *college* men soon. And you know who's gonna be in college *with* us?"

The blank expressions Jake and Ben and T.J. were wearing developed into looks of active confusion.

"Girls who . . . *used* to be in high school?" T.J. asked.

"No, man. *Women,*" Mike said, dropping his hamburger onto the tray before him. *"College* women. Women with no curfew and . . . women who party, and . . . *women,* bro! We're staring into the future, and it . . . is . . . *women!"*

Ben and T.J. turned to one another, grinning, and said simultaneously, "Women."

"I never thought about that," Jake said.

Mike nodded as he lifted his burger and took a large bite out of it. "I'm always a step ahead of you guys," he said with one cheek bulging. "That's why I play defense." He took another drink of his beer.

Mike's friends all lifted their burgers and took hefty bites, as well. There was a long moment of loud, wet, lip-smacking chewing between the four of them.

"Hey," Ben said, frowning. He looked deep in thought as he took a moment to suck his teeth and run his tongue beneath his lips. "Maybe we should dump *our* girlfriends, too." He looked around at his buddies.

Mike grinned. "Now, *that* would be *sweet!* We'd have the whole summer to just hang out together and party and chase every chick in sight! Without our lame girlfriends hanging around."

"Yeah," T.J. said, nodding. "They *hate* it when we chase other chicks."

"That's what I'm saying, guys!" Mike exclaimed. "They're just gonna hold us back. They're gonna keep us from hooking up with the *real* women that're gonna be all around us at college!"

Jake put a few fries in his mouth, chewed for a moment, then said, "You're right, Dex, man. I don't need that!"

Mike put an arm around Jake's shoulders and gave him a good, hard, macho squeeze. "Yes! That's my *man!* That's what I wanna *hear!*"

"Yeah," Ben said with two French fries hanging out of his mouth. "Me, too. I'm gonna break up with Cindi as soon as I see her tonight."

"All *right!*" Mike exclaimed, grinning. He pounded fists with Ben across the table in a moment of deep male bonding, as Ben and Jake both chewed noisily on their fries.

Mike, Jake, and Ben turned to T.J., who was slowly and thoughtfully lifting his hamburger to his mouth. He frowned as he took a big bite, then looked at his three friends.

"What if they start crying and stuff?" T.J. asked with his mouth full, frowning.

"Who *cares?*" Mike replied.

Two seconds went by before T.J. put his burger down and said, "Okay, you guys, I'm in."

Mike raised both arms in victory and shouted, *"Yes!"*

"This is *brilliant,* man!" Ben said. *"Such* a good idea!"

With his jaw set, Ben lifted his cup dramatically. Mike raised his, then Jake and T.J. did the same.

"Mike Dexter is a *god,"* T.J. said as their cups touched together.

"No, no," Jake said, turning to Mike. Jake raised his beer and the others joined him in a toast. In a low and very serious voice, Jake said, "Mike Dexter is a *role model."*

Chapter 3

"**M**IKE DEXTER'S AN ASSHOLE," WILLIAM LICHTER declared.

The basement of William's house was not really a basement at all. It was a secret underground *lair*.

The walls were covered with full-color seminude pictures of *Star Trek* stars Terry Farrell and Jeri Ryan, and *The X-Files* star Gillian Anderson. There were action figures and spaceship models on shelves and desktops and tabletops from all four *Star Trek* shows and all the *Star Wars* movies. There was a massive multimedia computer station set up on top of two pushed-together desks. It was big enough to bear a vague resemblance to the equipment on the bridge of a small starship.

In the middle of it all stood William Lichter. He was tall and skinny, with wildly uncombed brown hair and a pair of glasses that often slid down his nose. He stood in his dimly lit basement bathed in the blue-green glow of the computer station, wearing a blue polo shirt and gray pants, looking at a sheet of paper with an intense frown.

Seated at a table behind him were his two best friends in the world, Geoff Piccirilli and Murphy Pelan. Geoff was sitting at the computer station, surfing the Internet. Murphy sat near by, playing with the Luke Skywalker and Darth Vader action figures, speaking for both of them. They both wore *X-Files* T-shirts. Geoff's read, "The truth is out there," and Murphy's read, "Trust no one."

"Did you hear me?" William asked, turning to them.

Both of William's friends ignored him. Geoff continued to type on the computer keyboard, and Murphy moved the action figures around as he said, in a deep, throaty voice, "I *am* your *father, Luke!*"

William stepped over to the computer station and slapped a hand onto the desktop, shouting, "Hel*lo!*"

Geoff and Murphy looked up at him, startled.

William continued: "I *said* . . . Mike Dexter is an *asshole!* He's a knuckle-dragging half-wit who's been taking advantage of his physical superiority for *too* long! For the past decade, he has made a *hobby* of my pain. Witness Exhibit A."

He walked over to a shelf on the wall and pointed to a beautifully constructed, but irreparably damaged diorama of a forest.

"My eighth grade science project. A working rain forest, *perfectly* constructed, *completely* functional. Mike Dexter threw it out a third floor window." He sighed and shook his head. "It rains here no more, my friends."

William went to a sideboard, opened a drawer and removed a black eye patch. "Exhibit B. The eye patch I wore for three weeks after Mike beaned me with a raisin in home economics. It was cinnamon bun week."

He dropped the eye patch back in the drawer and removed a Ziploc bag bulging with the colorful, confetti-like remains of a comic book. "Exhibit C. My copy of the first issue of *Spawn*. Shredded by Mike. Street value: twenty dollars. Sentimental value: priceless." He dropped it back into the drawer. "Of course, there have been many other incidents, too numerous to recount here. Being tripped in the cafeteria, stripped of my swimming trunks in the pool. It goes on and on. But worst of all . . ." He took from the drawer a folded-up pair of pants, shook them out and held them up. There was an ugly brown stain on the backside between the pockets. "The Pudding Incident." He tossed the pants aside. "Need I say more?"

Geoff and Murphy shook their heads quickly.

William began to pace back and forth in front of his two friends, like a general pacing before his troops. "Tonight, gentlemen, Mike Dexter will know humiliation. Tonight, he will know ridicule. For *tonight* is the night we fight *back!* Tonight is"—he turned and faced them—*"Independence Night!"*

Geoff and Murphy looked at one another, eyes blinking rapidly, then turned to William again with blank expressions.

William's shoulders sagged as he sighed with frustration. "Okay, okay, maybe we should go over the plan one more time. I'm gonna be *depending* on you two! And frankly . . . it scares me. Okay, you guys, come over here."

Geoff and Murphy stood and followed William over to a table cluttered with magazines, model parts, and action figures.

"Now, pay attention, because this will only work if we're *totally* in synch." William cleared a space, then grabbed two action figures. "We'll set up in the backyard at the poolhouse . . . *here,*" he said, placing his hand flat on the tabletop. He stood two of the figures on the table and said, "Okay, Geoff, you're Grand Moff Tarkin, and Murphy, you're Boba Fett. Now, we're gonna have to—"

"How come *he* gets to be Boba Fett?" Geoff asked.

William rolled his eyes. "Okay, whatever. *He's* Grand Moff Tarkin and *you're* Boba Fett. Now, we're gonna—"

"Hey!" Murphy interrupted. "I don't wanna be Grand Moff Tarkin!"

"Okay, *fine!*" William barked. He went to a shelf, grabbed another action figure, and slapped it onto the table. "Geoff is Boba Fett, and *you,* Murphy, are Captain Picard!"

Murphy grinned and nodded. "Cool."

"Okay, is everybody happy now?" William asked.

Geoff and Murphy smiled and nodded.

"All right, then. At the predetermined time, I lead Mike and one of his random jock friends out to the poolhouse, where you guys are waiting on the roof.

You pounce down on them, render them unconscious with the chloroform we mixed in the chem lab." William stopped to point to a Thermos with the head of a *Tyrannosaurus rex* attached to the top of it. A small skull and crossbones had been taped on to the side. "Then," William continued, "we strip off their clothes and take Polaroids of said jocks in a lurid embrace. We see that the pictures are passed around at the party and . . . *boom*. We've got *instant* humiliation."

Geoff and Murphy laughed and gave their friend a round of applause.

"Hey, wait a second," Murphy said. "How are you gonna get them to follow you out to the poolhouse?"

William said, "I'm gonna tell them Melissa Greenspan and Ashley Haussman are making out together and want them to watch." William gave his friends a toothy grin.

"Cool," Murphy said.

"I'd go out to watch that," Geoff said.

"It's time to finally even the score with that troglodyte," William said. His grin was gone and his eyes were narrowed. "Revenge will be sweet. . . . And it will be *mine."*

William walked to a corner of the room and began gathering the supplies needed for the night's activity while Geoff and Murphy battled with their action figures.

"Okay," William said.

Geoff and Murphy both looked up to see William with a small satchel in his right hand, his other arm through the rungs of a ladder, and a camera hanging from his neck.

"Are we ready to move out?" William asked. "Let's *go!*"

William headed up the stairs, and Geoff and Murphy followed him.

"Jeez," Murphy said, "I wonder what it'll be like in there tonight . . . in that party, I mean. Y'know? I mean, you think people will be doing drugs?"

"Are you *kidding?*" Geoff replied as they headed up the stairs. "People may even be having *sex* in there tonight!"

Chapter 4

"I'VE *GOT* TO HAVE SEX TONIGHT."

Kenny Fisher stood at the magazine rack in his neighborhood convenience store with his friends "DJ" Sammy and Richie "Koolboy." All three of them had graduated from Huntington High that morning and were killing time before heading for the big graduation party.

All three boys wore clothes that were excessively baggy, especially their pants, which were worn low so a couple inches of their underwear were visible.

All three boys moved to a beat only they could hear, and waved their arms as they walked and talked.

And all three boys were white.

Kenny was thumbing through an adult magazine slowly, looking at the "Girls of the Pac Ten" through his large wraparound sunglasses. "I mean, peep *dis,* homeboys." He held out the magazine so Sammy and Richie could see the layout. "Ninety-two percent of the honeys at UCLA are sexually active. Ninety-two per*cent!* You know what *dat* means?"

Sammy took the magazine and he and Richie leaned their heads together to study the revealing pictures of beautiful coeds. If they knew what it meant they were keeping it to themselves.

"Dat means," Kenny said, stabbing a hand at the open magazine, "I got a ninety-two percent chance of embarrassing myself when I hook up wit' dat shortie and don't know twenny diff'rent ways to make her call me Big *Poppa,* dass what *dat* means." He adjusted the goggles he wore over his eyes.

Richie snatched the magazine from Sammy's hands, lifted it to his face, and slowly licked one of the pictures.

"Knock dat off!" Kenny said, grabbing the magazine back.

Sammy and Richie flanked him to stare at the pictures.

"Now you got *spit* all over dis fiiiine UCLA honey," Kenny grumbled, wiping the page with his sleeve.

"Dawg, dey's no *way* she goes to UCLA," Sammy said, pointing at the slightly moistened picture.

"It *says* so, don't it?" Kenny replied. "An' even if she *don't,* G, *every* girl in L.A. looks like dat. She probably be da *ugliest* girl in L.A.!"

"Awww, yeeaahh, Kenny, man," Richie said. "You gonna have all da mad honeys! I be jettin' out to yo' crib *every* weekend! You know what'm sayin'?"

"Word," Kenny said with a single nod. He handed the magazine to Sammy, turned and headed down one of the store's aisles, saying, "I gotta get some Breath Assure."

Richie followed him down the aisle and asked, "So what? Who's da lucky girl?"

"I haven't decided," Kenny said as he searched a shelf for breath freshener. "I figure since da whole class is goin' to da party, I should give all da ladies an equal chance. You know what'm sayin'?" He grabbed a box of the bad breath remedy, then turned to Richie. "Took me all day justa narrow it down to a list of ten *fine* finalists."

Richie held out his hand and smirked. "Lemme see."

Kenny reached over his shoulder into his vinyl backpack. He pulled out a small notebook, thumbed through it until he found the page he was looking for, then handed it over to Richie.

"I got a sophisticated rating scale," Kenny said, "including looks, body, reputation, might-owe-me-a-favor, and I—"

Richie threw back his head and burst into laughter. "Might owe you a favor? Aww, yeah, homeboy, *dat'll* work. 'Hey, Jenny, I know I let you cheat off me in math, so . . . you think I could stick my straw in your juicebox?'" He laughed again, loudly, shaking his head as he looked down at the notebook.

Kenny snapped the notebook from Richie's

hands, frowning. "Yo, why you don't show no love, brother? Check this . . . I am a *finesse* player, you know what'm sayin'? I am gonna Barry White my way into a woman's heart. Observe."

Kenny took off his backpack and held it before him as he unzipped it. It folded open in his arms like a large book.

"Da *Looooove* Kit," Kenny said.

The open backpack revealed a portable adult novelty store. The backpack contained a long strip of condoms folded into a stack, two containers of flavored massage oil, one coconut and one vanilla, and a CD titled *Between the Sheets*.

There was something else, as well, something very unusual . . . something long and pink. Richie reached for it quickly, and although Kenny tried to stop him, he wasn't fast enough. Richie removed the object from the open backpack and held it up for inspection. He grinned as he tilted it this way and that, looking it over carefully. Kenny grabbed for it, but Richie backed up a step and kept it out of his reach.

"What's this?" Richie asked in a loud, singsong voice.

Kenny jumped forward and snatched the long pink object from Richie's hand. He put it back in the backpack and folded it closed, pulling the zipper all the way around it.

"*Dat* was a 'Smell of Love' scented candle," Kenny said as he put the backpack on again. "And if either-a you knew anything at all about *seduc-*

23

tion . . . you'd know dat da honeys go wild for little romantic gestures like scented *candles*. So get outta my *face.*"

Kenny turned away from them and went to the register. Sammy and Richie exchanged a look, then followed.

The clerk was a tall young black man. He watched the three teenage boys approach the register, then he stared at Kenny for a long moment, and Sammy for a long moment, and Richie for a long moment.

They stared back at the cashier silently.

"Can I pay for this?" Kenny asked, putting the Breath Assure on the counter.

The cashier shook his head very slowly back and forth as he looked at them pathetically. "Yeah," he said finally, "at least your money's good."

Once Kenny had paid for the Breath Assure and stuffed it into a pocket, the three of them headed for the door.

"You actually think you're gonna go to dis party tonight armed with a my-first-time kit," Richie said, "and some honey's gonna let you do your first wit' her?"

With his hand on the metal bar that crossed the glass door, Kenny stopped and turned to his two friends. He smiled and said, "Just watch me, G."

Chapter 5

IT WASN'T HARD FOR PRESTON TO FIND THE PARTY. If he hadn't been to Molly Stinson's house before, the cars lining the street for blocks, the crowd in her front yard, and the loud music booming from her house all made it pretty obvious where the party was.

Molly lived in the wealthy neighborhood of Lawn-crest, which was populated by doctors, lawyers, and the owners of convenience stores. She had held quite a few parties over the last four years, so nearly everyone in the senior class had been to her house at least once.

But this party was different. It wasn't just another pool party or Halloween costume bash. This was the final blowout, the last time the seniors of Huntington High would ever party together. Oh, sure, there would be reunion parties where they would gather to see who got married, who got rich, and who got dumpy-looking, but it would not be the same. This party would mark the end of an era in their lives. This would be their last time gathered as fresh, young teenagers with the future spread out before them like a tremendous banquet. Tonight would be important, special. It would be a night for them to remember for the rest of their lives.

"Who's that throwing up in those tulips?" Denise asked.

"Can't tell," Preston said, turning to look out the passenger window. He drove slowly past Molly's house, looking from one side of the street to the other. The radio was playing with the volume low. "Jeez, it looks like the whole school's showing up."

"Fabulous," Denise drawled sarcastically.

Preston sighed and said, "You know, this is the last night of high school. You may want to at least *try* enjoying it."

"*Last* night was the last night of high school," Denise said, rolling her eyes. "This is just some desperate attempt for the winners to suck out every last drop of their glory days. Unaware that they're about to enter a world where popularity is not a free pass, and whatever good looks they have now won't go far . . . let alone last long." She wrinkled her nose and curled her upper lip, as if she'd just bitten into something that tasted foul. "I don't need to say good-bye to any of these people."

Preston shook his head and clicked his tongue. "So young, so bitter."

"Story of my life."

Preston pulled into a neighboring driveway to turn around. As he neared Molly's house again, he saw a tiny white hatchback pulling out of a parking space. The small car had a sign on top that read UPPER CRUST PIZZA.

"Ah-*hah!*" Preston exclaimed. "The pizzas have been delivered, and a parking space is open . . . *right* in front of the house!"

"You're gonna try to fit your car into that little cube of space?" Denise asked.

"Hey, it's an opening, okay?"

Preston carefully and slowly began to edge his vintage Cadillac into the small parking space. As he eased backward, then forward, then backward, again and again, he said, "You know, I, uh . . . brought the letter."

"You're *not* gonna give her the letter," Denise said.

"Why wouldn't I give her the letter?"

"Because you haven't had time to revise it . . . for the four *billionth* time."

"Hey, all great writers revise."

"Dear Amanda," Denise said in a whiny voice, "now that you're finally single I can finally give you the sappy love letter I never had the guts to give you during all four years of high school—"

"Yeah, yeah," Preston said, still working his way into the parking space, "go ahead and make fun. I don't care."

"I know. You don't care. *That's* what scares me, Pres."

Annoyed with her friend, Denise reached down

and turned on the radio. She started pressing buttons to change stations.

"Oh, *wait!*" Preston said, pulling her hand away from the radio. "Shh!"

Barry Manilow was singing "Mandy."

"What?" Denise asked. "It's Barry Manilow. Hey, why do you have a *preset* that plays Barry Manilow songs? Is this—oh, God—you listen to Mello One-Oh-Three?"

"'Mandy'!" Preston exclaimed. He'd managed to squeeze his car into the parking space. "That's it! 'Mandy,' *Amanda* . . . that's *it!* That's a *sign!*"

"Hey, Preston," Denise said, "I hate to disturb the alternate universe you've wandered into, but that song is supposedly about his dog."

"What?" Preston barked. "It's not about his *dog.* It's about a woman . . . named Amanda. Nobody names their *dog* Amanda."

"My cousins named their dog Samantha."

Preston turned off the engine, removed the key from the ignition, and stuffed it into his pocket. Leaning forward, he opened the glove compartment and removed *the* letter in its white envelope. He held it up and said, "Consider me ready."

Denise rolled her eyes as she got out of the car.

They followed the path that led to the front door, passing the crowd of chattering partyers on the front lawn. Preston reached out and pushed the doorbell.

Seconds later, the door opened and Molly faced them with a broad grin and eyes the size of silver dollars.

"Hiiiii!" she cried loudly, as if she'd been born deaf. "Come on in! But don't let the dog out!"

Preston and Denise both looked down to see a large, well-groomed sheepdog beside Molly. The dog was looking up at them, but it was impossible to tell if it was looking at Preston or Molly because of the hair over its eyes.

"Oh, my *God,* I'm *so* glad you came!" Molly exclaimed. "But don't let the dog out."

Preston and Denise smiled at Molly and moved past her.

They'd walked six steps into the house when they were rushed by a girl with long blond hair in pigtails, wearing a short, flouncy pink dress and a wild grin. It took him a moment, but Preston finally remembered her name: Vicki Compter.

"Preston *Meyers!*" Vicki cried. "Not one step *farther* until you sign my yearbook!" She offered her yearbook to Preston with one hand, a pen with the other.

"Uh . . . sure," Preston said, taking the yearbook and pen. He opened the book and looked for his picture.

"I'm going to be the first Huntington High student to get all five hundred and twenty-two seniors to sign my yearbook!" Vicki said proudly.

"Everybody's gotta have a dream," Denise replied.

Preston signed his picture and handed the yearbook and pen back to the girl.

"Denise *Fleming!*" Vicki cried, handing the yearbook and pen over to Denise. "I had to make a special little place for you to sign in the back because you didn't get your senior portrait taken." She lowered her head slightly and gave Denise a pouty look. *"Why* didn't you get your senior portrait taken?"

Denise thumbed her way to the back of the book, found the empty space, and scribbled her name.

"I didn't have my senior portrait taken," Denise said as she handed the yearbook and pen back to the girl, "specifically to avoid annoying and unpleasant moments like *this.*"

Vicki clutched her yearbook to her chest and shrieked, "Thank you so *much,* you two! Gooooooo *Huntington!*" She gave them a little jump, shot a fist into the air, and scurried away.

Preston and Denise turned to one another.

"Okay," Denise said, "I'm ready to leave."

"Would you *stop* it," Preston said. "This is our *graduation* party! Just because you meet one weird girl as soon as you walk in doesn't mean you have to *leave.* Okay?"

Denise shrugged and said, "Well . . ."

Mary Hampson, a girl with shoulder-length brown hair stumbled up to them and stopped. She stared at them for a long moment. Her face was red and puffy, as if she'd been crying, and she was so drunk she could hardly stand up. Preston and Denise stared back at her as she swayed from side to side.

The girl's face screwed up slowly. Tears began to flow freely from her eyes as her lips pulled back from her teeth. Sounds came from her mouth as her lips moved and her jaw worked. She was speaking . . . saying *something* . . . but it was unintelligible. "Thush bezt tea weveram sisu gizem chext ear."[1] She dove forward and wrapped her arms around both of them, squeezing them in a group hug. After a moment, she turned and hurried away with her hand over her teary eyes.

Once again, Preston and Denise looked at one another.

"There's one at every party," Preston said.

"Kinda makes you wanna never drink, huh?" Denise asked.

Preston laughed and nodded.

"Okay," Denise said. "I'm even *more* ready to leave now."

Preston frowned at her, grabbed her hand, and pulled as he started walking. "Just shut up and enjoy yourself, okay?" he said.

As Preston dragged her into the party, Denise tilted her head back and rolled her eyes.

---

[1]"This is the best party ever! I am gonna miss you guys so *much* next year!"

Chapter 6

KENNY HAD BEEN DRIVING HIS SHINY GREEN RANGE
Rover up and down the street, looking for a parking
space. Dr. Dre was pounding from the stereo speakers so loudly that the roots of Kenny's teeth vibrated
deep in his gums. Sammy was in the passenger seat
and Richie was in the back. Both of them were
moving their arms to the beat and reciting the lyrics
along with Dr. Dre.

It seemed like every inch of space had been filled
on both sides of the street, except for the unblocked
driveways. He pulled into one, then backed out and
headed back the way he'd come.

Kenny pulled his Rover into the only space in
front of Molly Stinson's house: directly in front of
her driveway. When he killed the engine, the stereo
shut off. For a moment, the silence was deafening as
Kenny's ears rang like cathedral bell towers.

All three boys sat in silence for a moment, jaws slack as each one stuck a finger in his ear and waggled it up and down rapidly. As Kenny got out, Sammy and Richie looked around to see where they were.

"Kenny, the girl is gonna *freak* if you park here," Richie said. "You're blockin' the whole *driveway!*"

Kenny turned back and said, "Yeah, well, she should have valet. Now, c'mon, les go. Time is honeys, homes."

Sammy and Richie got out and followed Kenny up the driveway, along the path by several outdoor partyers, and to the front door.

"Ladies, ax not for whom da bell tolls," Kenny said quietly. He reached out and rang the doorbell. "It be tollin' for you lucky girls."

A few seconds later, the door opened and Molly Stinson grinned out at them.

"Hi!" she gushed. "Oh, thank you so much for coming! Come on in!" She stepped back so they could come inside. As Kenny stepped through the door, she exclaimed, "But don't let the dog out, okay? Do *not* let the dog out!"

Kenny looked down at the the sheepdog. The dog stared up at him, eyes hidden behind mop-like strands of hair, long pink tongue bobbing in and out of its mouth.

"Hey, dog," Kenny said as Sammy and Richie came in behind him.

Something caught Molly's attention and she turned away from them. "Hey, you *guys,"* she called, stepping over to an open doorway. A tape barrier was fluttering to the floor. Molly picked it up and fixed it back in place.

Sammy and Richie flanked Kenny, leaving the front door wide open behind them.

"'Sup?" Sammy asked Kenny, who was still looking down at the dog.

"I dunno," Kenny said. "Dis dog be givin' me da eye."

Suddenly, the sheepdog dove for Kenny and jumped up on him. The dog planted two big front paws on Kenny's chest and began licking his face with long, wet, sloppy strokes.

"Huh-huh-*hey!*" Kenny sputtered. "Chuh-*chill, dog, chill!*"

Molly turned away from the door and spoke loudly to no one in particular. *"Seriously,* people, no one's allowed in this room, okay? My parents get home on Sunday and I don't want—" She turned as she spoke and saw the dog jumping all over Kenny. Then she saw the open front door. *"Hey!"* Molly cried. "Don't let Mister Tuxford out!"

"Get *off* me, you-you-you *dog!*" Kenny snapped, pushing at the dog. His face was glistening with sheepdog saliva. *"Yo!* Go away! Get outta here!"

Molly Stinson's sheepdog, Mr. Tuxford, dropped to the floor and did exactly as he'd been told. He ran out the front door.

"No!" Molly screamed. "Mister Tuxford, *no!* Mister Tuxford! Mister *Tuxford,* get *back* here!" She ran to the open door and stared out into the night. "Stop him! Somebody stop my *dog!*" But none of the partyers on the lawn listened to her. Most of them

were too wasted to know what she was talking about. Mr. Tuxford ran right by them, unnoticed. "Oh, *great!* Mister *Tux*ford, *come!*" When the dog didn't respond, Molly ran after him.

Kenny wiped at his face frantically with both hands, muttering, "Got me some *dog spit."* Finally, he stopped wiping, glanced at Sammy and Richie, and said, "C'mon, les jam before she comes back."

They made their way deeper into the house, but they didn't get far.

"Kenny *Fisher!*" Vicki Compter squealed as she rushed Kenny, holding out her yearbook. "Oh, *please* sign my yearbook!"

Kenny didn't stop walking. "No, thanks," he said, "no time."

Vicki's smile fell away as she turned to Sammy and Richie, who followed a step behind Kenny.

"Come *on!*" she cried. "Where's your school spirit?" She grinned again and started a cheer: " *'Who's* the *school* that's *num*-ber *one? Shout* it, *shout* it, *Hunt*-ing—'"

"Yo, get a *life,"* Richie said as they walked by her.

Sammy laughed and knocked fists with Richie, saying, "Awww, *yeah!*"

Vicki Compter's face fell as she watched the boys walk away. Her shoulders sagged and she released a long, sad sigh . . . until she turned around and saw another student walking through the front door. Suddenly, her grin returned as she ran forward, crying, "Oh, *please* sign my yearbook!"

Kenny entered the living room, with Sammy and Richie right behind him. Music was playing loudly on the stereo, a few people were dancing, and there was a lot of chattering and laughing going on.

"Awww, yeeaahhh," Kenny said, smiling as he nodded his head slowly. "Got lotsa crazy talent here tonight. Da shorties gonna be linin' up to get wit' da Kenster." He turned around to face Sammy and Richie. "Check you later, homes. Time to work my magic . . . time to do my bidness . . . time to work da list." He smiled, then turned and headed into the crowd.

Sammy and Richie didn't move. They stood in the doorway watching Kenny walk away, then they turned to one another.

"Think he's gonna hizzit the skizzins?" Sammy asked.

"I got *much* doubt," Richie said.

"Look out, coming through!" a voice said loudly behind them.

Sammy and Richie separated, clearing the doorway, and a dark-haired guy dragging an amp by the handle walked between them.

"Watch it, fellas," he said. He paused briefly to nod to each of them. "I'm with the band." Then he walked on, making his way through the crowd of partyers.

"Yo, *white* boy!" Sammy called after him. *"Check yo'self!"*

The guy with the band ignored the remark. His name was Jimmy Clark. He was the guitarist for the band that was to play at Molly Stinson's big graduation party. Jimmy walked to the far end of the living room, where the rest of the band was gathered. All

36

the furniture had been pushed aside and a small stage-like platform had been set up to elevate the band a couple feet above everyone else. The instruments, and the band members, were all ready. Jimmy plugged in the amp, then stood and turned to the lead singer, Walter Hall, who insisted that everyone call him The Wall.

"Man, our first show *ever!*" Walter exclaimed pacing excitedly. "This is gonna be *sweet!*"

Jimmy grinned and slapped hands with the drummer, Dan Schmidt, and the bass player, Brian Boyd. They had to speak loudly to be heard over the sounds of the party.

"Dude," Dan said, stepping in front of Walter, "I heard Carol Gronner invited her cousin tonight."

Walter stopped and stared at him for a moment. *"So?"*

Dan continued: "Well, his brother's roommate knows a guy who knows a *scout!* Out in *L.A.!*"

"Get *out!*" Brian exclaimed.

"I'm serious, dudes," Dan said. "Serious as a heart attack."

Walter planted his fists on his hips, elbows jutting out at his sides, and frowned as he nodded slowly, and very seriously. "That's good. Glad we got those T-shirts printed."

The T-shirts were piled in a corner of the living room. It was a *huge* pile of neatly folded white shirts; on the front of each was the band's name, SOUND-BURGER, between two sesame seed buns. The pile consumed the entire corner of the room.

They'd been practicing in Walter's garage for four

years, writing songs, perfecting their sound, working on their image. This party was their first exposure. It could very well determine the entire future of the band.

"Hey, um, I'm just wondering, Walter," Brian said. "You think maybe we had too many of them shirts made? Maybe?"

Walter closed his eyes for a moment as he sucked in a deep breath through clenched teeth. His eyes opened and glared at Brian as he spoke in a low, threatening voice through still-clenched teeth: "Man, how many *times* do I have to *tell* you . . . I am The *Wall!* That's what you *call* me! That's my *name!* It's like The Edge, y'*know?* That's who I *am,* and that's what you *call* me!"

"Oh, yeah, yeah, right." Brian bowed his head, shook it rapidly with frustration, and stomped a foot. "I *forgot,* man. Sorry. So . . . you think maybe we made too many of them shirts?"

"No *way,* man," Walter said. "We're gonna *shine* tonight. And all these partyers? They're gonna be *craving* any piece of us they can *get!* When we leave here tonight, I guarantee you . . . we won't have any shirts *left!"*

"Then what're we waiting for?" Jimmy asked, reaching down and lifting his guitar from its case. "Let's get this show on the road!"

Chapter 7

"**L**ET'S GO, GUYS."

The party had not yet spread to Molly Stinson's backyard. Lights along the edge of the roof illuminated the pool and reflected off the surface of the water, landing on the back walls of the house as fluttering, fragmented apparitions. The thumping beat of the music playing on the stereo inside came through the walls, but the backyard was still and silent.

William crept across the lawn beyond the pool, avoiding the light. Halfway to the poolhouse, he crouched down and quickly looked around.

William lifted his arm and waved, letting Murphy and Geoff know that the coast was clear. Then he hurried the rest of the way to the poolhouse. Moments later, he was joined by Murphy and Geoff.

William still carried the small satchel in his right

hand, still had the Polaroid camera swinging from around his neck, and still had his left arm through a tall ladder. At the poolhouse, he put the satchel down and leaned the ladder against the side of the low building.

"Okay, this is it," William said very quietly, looking at Geoff and Murphy as he gestured toward the ladder.

Geoff and Murphy stood side by side, looking at William. They looked up at the roof of the poolhouse, then at William again.

Geoff licked his lips, gulped once, and raised his arm to point up at the roof. "Up thuh-*there?*" he whispered hoarsely.

"It's barely six feet off the *ground,*" William hissed insistently.

Geoff nodded and said, "Yeah, but do you know what kind of injuries a body can sustain from falling just six feet?"

William sighed as he ran a hand through his hair, frustrated. "C'mon, guys, look: It's just like the episode where Mulder had to climb up the water tower to check out that abduction site. Remember?"

Murphy reached up and absently massaged his neck. "Oh, yeah, that's right," he whispered, turning to Geoff. "Episode twenty-three. 'The Erlenmeyer Flask.' Remember?"

"Oh, yeah," Geoff replied, nodding slowly. "I guess so."

A long, silent moment passed. Geoff and Murphy looked at each other, then at William, then at each other again. Finally, Geoff stepped over to the ladder. He reached out and clutched one of the rungs with two hands, testing its sturdiness.

"Okay," Geoff breathed. "For Mulder." He began climbing the ladder, slowly and cautiously, finally picking up speed on the last three rungs. He looked down at them from the poolhouse roof, a little more confident now. "C'mon up, Murph."

Murphy climbed the ladder and joined Geoff on the roof.

"Okay, you guys," William said, *"catch."* He took the camera from around his neck and tossed it up. Geoff caught it neatly. "Here, Murphy," he said, tossing the satchel up. Murphy caught it, set it aside, then looked down and nodded. "All right, are you guys set?" William asked. "We'll rendezvous at twenty-four-thirty." They all checked their watches. "I'm goin' in."

William began moving his head around in slow circles as he tensed his shoulders and loosened them, tensed them and loosened them. He was trying to relax himself, loosen up, get ready to face the enemy.

"Wait, William!" Murphy hissed. "If you're goin' in there . . . well, I mean . . . there's gonna be *drinking* in there!"

"Yeah," William said. "So?"

"Well, what're you gonna *do?*" Murphy replied. "They're gonna kick you out if you don't drink!"

"Oh, but I *will* be drinking!" William said. "I'll *have* to! It's all part of my cover, Murphy. I can't just go in there and wander around like a *dork!* I've *got* to drink. You know the old saying 'when in Rome . . .'?"

Geoff and Murphy looked at one another for a moment, then back down at William.

"Rome?" Geoff asked. "What's Rome got to do with anything?"

Murphy's whole face screwed up as he asked, "Are you saying you're gonna become a *Catholic?*"

William sighed and waved his arms. "Forget Rome, okay? Just *forget* it."

"But, William," Geoff said, "if you go in there and drink, you could . . . well, you could get *drunk!*"

"You could get *addicted!*" Murphy added.

William gave them a confident smile and shook his head reassuringly. "Don't worry, I've taken care of that," he whispered up at them. He removed a piece of paper from his pocket. It was folded into a tiny square. Unfolding it revealed a computer-printed chart. "In order to not blow my cover," William continued, holding the chart up for them to see, "I devised a formula whereby I can monitor my blood alcohol level. I know *exactly* how many spirits I can imbibe without affecting my behavior or judgment." He folded the chart up quickly and slipped it back into his pocket. "That way, I'll be able to drink and fit in, but *without* screwing up our plan."

Geoff and Murphy stared down at William slack-jawed for a moment.

"Wow," Geoff whispered respectfully. "You've got every angle covered, William."

Murphy had to move his mouth a few times before he found his voice. When he spoke, it was with great reverence: "Just like Cancer Man."

William blinked with surprise. "Jeez, thanks,

Murphy," he said, a smile growing slowly on his face. "That's . . . y'know, that's quite a compliment." He glanced at his watch, then straightened his shoulders and took in a deep, steadying breath. "Okay," he said, "I guess it's . . . time."

"Good luck, man," Murphy said.

"Thanks." William turned and started for the house, but stopped and turned back when Geoff hissed his name.

"William," Geoff said, "remember: Trust no one."

William nodded once, then turned and walked away, heading for the back patio. A knot of excitement tightened in his gut as he got closer to the back door of the house. Four long years of torment and humiliation: four years of being tripped in the cafeteria, being given public wedgies, being called every conceivable dehumanizing name, getting his head shoved in toilets, and countless other heinous tortures. . . . All of that was about to be avenged.

William wasn't the only one to suffer at the hands of Mike Dexter and his simian friends, but he'd certainly suffered the most. He'd decided from the inception of his plan that it would not only be revenge for himself, but for *all* of Mike Dexter's victims. It would be a victory for everyone who had ever been picked on by the biggest *jock* on campus. And William was going to be the one to do it. He would get no credit for it, there would be no thanks from those who benefitted from it, but that was okay. He was going to do it because it *had* to be done . . . and because it was his destiny to do it.

He crossed the pool area, walked along a flagstone path to the house and stopped at the back door. Music played inside and voices laughed and chattered. Steeling himself, William opened the door and went inside . . . to his destiny.

The party was well underway and was growing louder by the minute as more people arrived. In the foyer of the house, several grinning, laughing students had gathered around Olaf Van Hermert, a gangly foreign exchange student from Belgium. He had a lopsided haircut and wore jeans and a T-shirt that read USA on the front.

Olaf had spent the last few months of his senior year at Huntington High, and that morning, he had graduated with a whole lot of other students who were, essentially, total strangers. It had been difficult for him to get to know any of them because Olaf had not yet quite mastered English. In fact, he was very *far* from mastering it. But he was pleased by how friendly the American students were, especially the ones surrounding him at that very moment. They were taking the time, in the middle of a party, to teach him the finer points of their language.

"I am a-a-a," Olaf said. He spoke haltingly, and with a very thick Belgian accent. The others were telling him what to say, and he was repeating the words as best he could. One sentence at a time, he was *learning!* Olaf shook his head and started over again. "I am . . . a . . . sex machine."

The others laughed hysterically and clapped their hands. Olaf beamed proudly.

"Let's teach him something else!" Flower Kowalski said to her boyfriend, Eddie Wright.

Flower and Eddie were always referred to as "the hippie couple" by everyone at Huntington. They both had long, stringy hair of indeterminate color and both wore clothes so out of date they seemed to have been purchased at a clearance sale in the middle of a time warp. Their eyes were always only half open, and they drove around in Eddie's beat-up old Volkswagen van, which looked like it belonged in a museum of ancient history. On top of that, they were always smiling and happy. Everyone assumed that was because they were always stoned.

"Okay, okay," Eddie said, his head bobbing up and down as he grinned. "Let's see. Uh . . . how about . . ." He turned to Olaf as the front door opened.

Mike, Jake, Ben, and T.J. walked into the house, and T.J. closed the door behind them. Mike lifted his arms in the air, fists clenched, tilted his head back and bellowed, "Huntington Hills Hiiiigh, you can *kiss my aaaassss!* Woo-*hooo!*"

Most of the students gathered around Olaf turned away to greet Mike and his friends. High fives were exchanged and loud greetings were shouted. But Flower and Eddie remained with Olaf.

"Okay, Olaf, try this one," Flower said. " 'Take me, you love beast! I'm yours!' "

As if from nowhere, Vicki Compter appeared, yearbook in one hand, pen in the other, grinning widely. "Oh, my *God!*" she cried, stopping in front of Mike. "Mike *Dexter!* I've *got* to get you to sign my yearbook!"

Mike stepped around Vicki without giving her a glance. "C'mon, guys," he said, nodding for his three friends to follow him.

Vicki jumped directly in front of him, bringing him to a halt. He noticed her this time and frowned as she began bouncing around and broke into a cheer.

"'Which team has the winning play?'" she chanted. "'*Hunt*ington, *Hunt*ington, hey, hey—'"

Mike put a hand on her shoulder and gave her a good shove, then walked on with his friends.

Vicki slammed into a wall with a thud and whined, *"Hey."*

Laughing at Vicki, Jake, Ben, and T.J. high-fived one another.

Mike and his friends went into the living room, where Mike stopped and looked around.

"Dudes," he said. "There they are." He nodded toward three girls standing together a few yards away.

They were all blond and curvaceous and giddy as dental patients under gas. Beth, Cindi, and Debi: girlfriends of Jake, Ben, and T.J., respectively. Chronic perkiness would not allow them to stand still, and they frequently bounced up and down on the balls of their feet, always simultaneously, as if they'd rehearsed the move.

As he watched the girlfriends, Mike realized for the first time how very important it was to him that his buddies break up with them. Cindi, Debi, and

Beth were neither as cool nor as craved as Amanda, of course. There had been only one Amanda at Huntington. But they were ladies in waiting, the next best *thing* to Amanda, and they were all attached to his buddies. Mike had broken up with Amanda, so it was only right that his friends do the same with *their* girlfriends. It would be an example of Mike's influence, for one thing. And it would show that he had been *right* in doing what he'd done.

"Look at 'em," Mike said. Jake, Ben, and T.J. quickly gathered around and leaned in close to hear what he was saying. "They're *poodles*. You know what kinda people own poodles? Losers. Nobodies. And little old ladies with blue hair." He looked from Jake to Ben to T.J. "You guys are *poodle* owners right now, y'know that? You're losers. *Nobodies*. You're about to embark on the greatest adventure of your lives: *college!* And you're chained to *poodles!* Now, do you remember the agreement we made just a little while ago? Do you remember our *pact?*"

"I remember," Jake said. "And I plan to stick to it."

"Me, too, man," T.J. said.

Ben's eyes widened as he said, "I can't believe you'd *doubt* me, dude!"

"Good," Mike said with a grin. "Then let's go. You guys know what you have to do."

They headed through the crowd to the girlfriends, confident and determined.

But the night was still young.

Chapter 8

PRESTON AND DENISE STOOD TOGETHER NEAR THE fireplace, watching the party. Neither of them had done any dancing or mingling yet. They hadn't even gotten anything to drink. They'd just been . . . observing. Denise wore a flat expression of boredom, while Preston's eyes darted around the room, looking for Amanda, just in case she'd walked in while he wasn't looking.

"Well," Preston said, leaning close to Denise, "what do you think so far?"

Denise slowly lifted a single brow. "So far," she said, "I think this is Charles Darwin's idea of hell."

"Oh, come on," Preston said with a smirk. "Everybody's just having fun. Remember that? *Fun?*"

She ignored him and continued scanning the

room, until she spotted Mike moving through the crowd with his three friends.

"Oh, goodie," Denise said. "Look who's here. The Locker Room Brain Trust."

Preston followed her gaze until he saw them, too. He wondered how Amanda would feel if she arrived and found that Mike was there. Maybe she wouldn't come at *all*.

No, that can't happen, Preston thought. *Not tonight. Not after everything that's happened . . . after all the signs. She has to come tonight. We're meant to be together. It's fate. It's . . . it's destiny!*

Preston watched Mike and his buddies cross the room to join Cindi, Debi, and Beth. He leaned toward Denise again and said, "I wonder what they're saying."

"Nothing with multiple syllables, I promise you," Denise replied.

All three girls rushed to their boyfriends with arms open and outstretched.

"Theeerrrre you are!" Beth squealed, embracing Jake. "I missed you *soooo* much!"

Cindi ran forward and threw herself on to Ben, crying, "I haven't seen my boyfriend in six whole *hours!"*

Debi held back, though. She stood in front of T.J. with her arms open wide, stuck her lower lip out as far as it would go and said, "Come give your wuvvy bunny a *hug!"*

Mike felt his mouth quivering into a sneer as he

watched his buddies hug and kiss the girlfriends and return their affectionate cooings. They really *were* as disgusting as poodle owners, talking baby talk to their poofy, spoiled pets. Mike hoped they wouldn't forget the pact.

When they were done making spectacles of themselves and their boyfriends, Beth, Cindi, and Debi turned to face Mike. Their smiles fell away and they said nothing as they glared at him coldly.

"How ya doin'?" Mike said with a nod.

"How *could* you, Michael?" Cindi hissed.

"How could I *what?*" Mike asked, flinching. "And the name is *Mike,* if you don't mind." He hated being called Michael.

"You know what she's talking about," Beth said, folding her arms tightly across her chest.

"We *all* know what she's talking about," Debi added.

Mike frowned and fidgeted, then turned to his buddies, leaning close. "Dudes, remember the game plan," he said as quietly as possible.

"Uh, right," Jake said, nodding. He turned to Beth. "Look, we've gotta talk. In fact, uh . . . well, we've *all* gotta talk. Right guys?" He turned to Ben and T.J., but they weren't paying the least bit of attention to him. Instead, they were staring across the room. So was Mike, in fact. And so were Beth, Cindi, and Debi.

Everyone was turning to the other side of the room, and the din of voices rapidly quieted to a low rumble.

Debi gasped and whispered, "I can't believe she actually *came!*"

Amanda Beckett had just entered the room, and as usual, everyone had noticed. But this time it was different, because Mike was there, too . . . and everyone knew he'd broken up with her that morning.

Mike was *glad* Amanda had come to the party. If she was there, everyone would be reminded of exactly how gorgeous and desirable she was . . . and how unbelievably cool and confident Mike was to let her go. He stuffed his hands into his back pockets and grinned as Amanda walked into the room.

"Well, there she is," Denise said to Preston. "If you want, I can run and get a cup."

Preston tore his eyes away from Amanda for just a moment to glance at Denise with a frown. "What? A *cup?*"

"You know, to catch your brain when it dribbles out your ear."

Preston ignored her and looked at Amanda again, watching her walk into the crowd of partyers. Things quieted just a bit, and everyone stepped aside to let her through, parting like the Red Sea for Moses.

As usual, Amanda was breathtakingly beautiful. She wore a light blue tank top, a short matching skirt and heels. Her long, auburn hair fell over her shoulders in silky, glowing waves, and her eyes sparkled. She smiled at others as she passed them, showing no sign that she'd been dumped by her boyfriend that morning, even though Preston was certain that *she* knew that everyone *else* knew. She was not only an angelic vision, she was the personification of real, genuine, solid-gold class.

Preston heard Denise say something to him, but her voice was distant and her words indistinct. All the noise in the room—the thundering music, the voices, the laughter—fell to a dull, underwater garble. Preston straightened his posture and took the letter from his pocket. With determination in his eyes, he shouldered his way through the crowd toward Amanda and stepped in front of her.

She gave him a quizzical look, tilting her head slightly to one side as he handed her the letter. She seemed confused as she opened it and began to read. Her expression changed slowly as her eyes moved back and forth over the page. Her lovely features relaxed and her eyes widened just a bit. Her eyes glistened as tears formed, and finally spilled out and ran down her cheeks in graceful, sparkling rivulets. Her beautiful brown eyes rose slowly from the letter, until she was looking at Preston.

Unable to hold still, Preston shifted his weight from one foot to the other, back and forth, and stammered nervously for a moment. "Uh, look, I-I-I . . . Amanda, I—"

"Call me Mandy," she said.

Suddenly, from *somewhere,* Barry Manilow began to sing "Mandy."

Amanda allowed the letter to slip from her fingers and fall to the floor as she stepped forward and put her arms around Preston. Their lips grew closer and closer . . . but she stopped.

"Preston," she said. But there was something wrong with her voice. "Pres? *Preston!*" It wasn't Amanda's voice at all. It was *Denise's* voice! "Are you *high*, you dolt?"

Preston's entire body jerked as he came out of his fantasy. He had not walked over to Amanda, had not given her the letter. He hadn't even moved. He was still standing beside Denise, who was staring at him as if he were crazy. And Amanda was still across the room.

"Are you *with* us, Preston?"

"Uh, yeah, yeah, sure," he said, nodding. He watched Amanda disappear into the crowd.

"Well, there she goes," Denise said. She patted him on the back. "That was good. I think you made a real *connection* there."

"Very funny," Preston said, turning to her with a sad look in his eyes.

Denise's hand was still on his back, but instead of patting, she rubbed affectionately. "Hey, Pres. Don't look so down, okay? Tell you what, let's go get a drink. C'mon, off to the kitchen."

With an arm around his waist, Denise led Preston through the crowd, out of the living room, and down the hall to the kitchen.

Matt Schwartz was ahead of them in the hall. He was carrying a huge watermelon on his shoulder. They followed him into the kitchen.

"Hey, everybody!" Matt shouted. "I poured *six*

bottles of vodka into this watermelon last September, and it's been in my freezer *all year!*"

The partyers in the dining room suddenly rushed toward Matt, cheering wildly.

"Hey, wait," Matt said as they crowded around him smotheringly. He tried to move away from the enthusiastic vodka-melon fans. *"Wait* a second, or I'm gonna—"

Matt let out a yelp as he tripped and stumbled backward.

The melon shot into the air . . . and dropped to the floor with a wet *splat!,* spreading cold pink, aged vodka all over the tile floor.

Matt stared down at the shattered melon, eyes bulging, mouth gaping, and made unintelligible throaty sounds. The crowd that had gathered around him so quickly dispersed even faster, going back to the other rooms.

"Oh, now, *that* is truly tragic," Denise said sadly as she and Preston stepped over the mess.

Preston looked back toward the living room, eyes searching for Amanda.

"God, did you see how she looked?" he asked. "She's *beautiful.* Is it"—he turned to Denise—"Do you think it's possible she's gotten more beautiful since graduation?"

"I really don't think so, Pres," Denise said as she grabbed a cup and got some beer from the keg. As she turned around, she glanced down the hallway.

Just outside the kitchen, Kenny Fisher was standing in the hall before a mirror. He was practicing facial expressions, his body moving to a beat only he could hear as he moved his arms stiffly, jerkily, like a rap singer.

Denise nudged Preston with an elbow, and he turned to see her smiling as she looked out into the hall. She pointed, and Preston looked, saw Kenny posturing in front of the mirror.

In a high-pitched, girlish voice, Denise said, "Oh, God, when will I *ever* be on *Soul Train?*"

"Jeez," Preston said, turning away. "Do you have to rag on *everybody?*" He leaned on the counter and kept looking for Amanda.

"Oh, *please,* Preston," Denise said, rolling her eyes. "His wardrobe *alone* leaves him open for public mockery."

"Whatever you say. *I'm* not the one who used to sleep over at his house."

"Hey, that was in *fourth grade,*" Denise protested. "You wanna start going over who your friends were in fourth grade?"

Preston continued looking into the crowd. "So, do you see her anywhere? Where do you think she went?"

"Right over there," Denise said, pointing.

Preston followed her finger and saw Amanda joining her friends Beth, Cindi, and Debi. He grabbed Denise's arm and pulled it down, saying, "Well, don't *point* at her!"

"She didn't see," Denise assured him.

"C'mon, c'mon, *quick!*" Preston hissed as he pulled her out of sight of the partyers in the living room. He leaned against the refrigerator, closed his eyes, and took several deep breaths.

"Are you hyperventilating?" Denise asked. "Should I get a bag?"

"No, no, I . . . I'm centering myself. Harnessing my Ch'i."

Denise squinted at him, pulling her head back. "Were you this weird when we went out?"

Preston opened his eyes and faced her. "Were you this *bitchy* when we went out?"

"Yes, I was," she replied, nodding. "For the whole week. One bitchy little eighth grader."

"Okay, okay, I can do this," he said, pushing himself away from the refrigerator. "Look, are you gonna be okay here?"

"Yeah, sure, whatever," Denise said, shrugging one shoulder. "I think I'm gonna get a ride home with someone else though, seeing how you're probably gonna wanna stay later than me."

"Are you sure?"

"Sure, sure, I'm sure." She slapped his shoulder. "You go on. I'll see you later."

Preston nodded, then went into the crowded dining room and started to make his way through the crowd back into the living room.

Denise sighed as she looked over at all the other partyers. They were laughing and shouting at each other. Some were dancing.

They were *all* having fun.

She realized it was a lot more fun with Preston.

Without him, it was . . . kind of lonely.

Chapter 9

AMANDA JOINED BETH, CINDI, AND DEBI. MIKE AND his buddies were with them, but Amanda didn't care. She didn't care at all.

"Hey, guys," she said.

A wave of mumbled greetings came from the guys, but the girls were much more enthusiastic.

"It's *so* good to see you, Amanda," Debi said in a sad voice.

Beth stepped forward and hugged her. "We think it's *so* cool that you came tonight."

"Yeah, Amanda," Cindi said, "that really is cool. You are the *best.*"

Amanda found it a little annoying that her friends were treating her so gently, as if she'd just come back from having her dog put to sleep, or something. She'd seen them that afternoon and she'd tried hard to convince them that she was not devastated by the fact that Mike had broken up with her. Far *from* it. But they hadn't listened. Apparently, *they* would be devastated if Jake, Ben, or T.J. dumped them, so they figured she felt the same way. She didn't, though. Not at all.

Amanda turned to the guys and smiled, then met Mike's eyes and said, "Hey, Mike. How's it goin'?"

Suddenly, Amanda found herself surrounded by statues as Beth and Jake, Cindi and Ben, and Debi and T.J. froze.

Mike looked at Amanda for a moment, then his mouth curled in a sneer as he chuckled coldly. He turned away and looked around at the party, as if searching for someone more interesting.

Amanda rolled her eyes and sighed, never losing her smile. It was exactly what she'd expected from Mike. Suddenly, she didn't want to be anywhere near him, and she didn't want to be around her friends, who seemed to think he was so important to her that she couldn't cope with their breakup. She turned and walked away, moving into the crowd, hoping to have a good time.

"Now look what you did, Mike!" Beth exclaimed.

He looked at her with a smirk.

"Can't you see she's in pain?" Debi snapped.

Cindi stomped a foot and said, "God, do you think you could be a bigger jerk, Michael?"

"Mike," he growled.

"We'd better go talk to her," Beth said.

"Totally," Cindi agreed. "She looks destroyed."

"Suicidal!" Debi added.

Moving as one, the girls turned and kissed their boyfriends simultaneously.

"We'll be right back," Beth said. She glowered at Mike. "Way to go, asshole."

The three of them walked away, following the path through the crowd taken by Amanda.

Mike turned to his three buddies and grinned. "So! Where's the alcohol?"

Kenny was still standing in front of the mirror. But not for long. He'd decided it was time to go find his woman, to make his mark . . . to meet his destiny. He made sure his hair was perfect, then turned away from the mirror.

"Okay," he muttered to himself, "dis is it. Iss finally time for Kenny Fisher to become da *man*. I done my laps, I done my time." He stopped and removed his notebook from a pocket, opened it up, and looked at the list.

Kenny leaned into the kitchen door and looked inside, looking beyond it to the dining room. He spotted two of the girls on his list and smiled, nodding, mentally checking off the names. He went down the hall, stopped at an open doorway, and looked into the den, where he saw two more of the girls on his list. In the foyer, he went to a doorway where a tape barrier had been knocked down and leaned into a very fancy, expensively decorated room. There were two more of the girls in there. He grinned as he made his way into the living room. Six down, four to go.

Most of the partyers were gathered in the living room, which was the loudest part of the house. He looked around as he stumbled and pushed through the crowd. There was another of the girls on his list . . . and another . . . and another . . . and all *four* remaining girls were in the living room! They were *all* there!

Kenny leaned on the back of the sofa, looking at his list, muttering to himself, "All ten finalists are present and accounted for. Ten *fine* ladies . . . each one at my disposal. Ten willing and able tour guides into da theme park of *looove.* But who's it gonna be? Which of you gorgeous ten will be da lucky *one?*"

He looked up from his list just in time to see Corinne Emery coming toward him. She was the *first* name on his list and she was heading straight *for* him! It was fate. It *had* to be! He pushed away from the sofa and stuffed his notebook back into his pocket. Putting on his best smile, Kenny said, "Yo, Corinne!"

She turned to him, expressionless, still walking.

"You be lookin' *fine* t'night," he said. "Whass*up,* baby?"

She did not even pause; she just kept walking.

Kenny's eyes remained frozen on the spot where she'd been before she passed him up. He began to nod slowly as he removed his notebook from his pocket along with a stubby little pencil. He crossed Corinne's name off the list.

"Nine fine ladies," he muttered to himself. "Which of you gorgeous nine babes is gonna be da

one to accompany me into da bee-*yoo*-tiful land o' love?"

Corinne Emery walked right past Wiliam Lichter.

After squeezing himself through the treacherous, smothering field of bodies in the living room, William found himself in the foyer. People were coming and going all around him. He'd been bumping into people ever since he'd entered the house, and he'd apologized to each and every one of them. He ducked into the hallway to get his bearings.

He'd never seen anything like it. Dancing and shouting . . . the smell of alcohol and smoke permeating everything. He walked down the hall and looked into an open doorway. The kitchen. It was crowded and busy, but the smell of beer was strong. It *had* to be where everyone was getting their drinks.

Although he didn't want to, William knew he *had* to go in there and get a cup of beer. It was the only way he could solidify his cover.

William had no illusions about himself. He knew that he was a geek. The only way he could get through the party and be accepted would be with a cup of beer in his hand.

He walked up to the people gathered at the counter, stood up straight, cleared his throat, and asked, "Um, excuse me, please, but . . . is this the *beer?*"

The entire group parted and turned to look at him. Each person held a cup of beer.

One guy stood at the keg. A big, muscular guy with

short dark hair. He wore jeans and a T-shirt, and his muscles appeared ready to rip through them both.

"What does it *look* like?" the keg guy asked.

"Oh, yeah, right. Sorry." William gave the big guy his best smile.

The keg guy asked, "Do you *want* one, or *what?*"

"Oh, yeah, sure!" William blurted. "Of *course* I want one! That's why I'm here! I mean, heh-heh, that's why we're *all* here, right? Yeah, *sure!* Uh . . . gimme a beer!"

The keg guy filled a cup for him and handed it over. William tried to look casual as he took it.

While there was a lot of noise coming from the living room and dining room, William suddenly realized that everyone in the kitchen was silent . . . and staring at him. They were waiting for him to drink his beer.

He smiled at all of them bravely, lifted his cup and said, "Well, cheers." He sipped the beer . . .

. . . And immediately spit it out in a spray.

"My *God!*" he shouted. "Nobody *drink* this! It's *awful!* I-I-I think it's gone *bad!*"

Almost at once, everyone around him drank some of their beer.

"Tastes like beer to me," a girl said.

"Me, too," a guy said.

The keg guy said, "Mine's fine, too. What's your problem, boy?"

There was a long, ugly silence. William wondered if he were having a nightmare. He'd certainly had plenty of nightmares *like* this.

Suddenly, the silence was broken when someone

asked, "Hey, aren't you the guy who went in his pants in the cafeteria freshman year?"

Panic consumed William at the mention of the chocolate pudding incident. Burning under the gaze of so many people, he put the cup to his mouth and began gulping frantically. He pulled the empty cup away from his mouth with a gasp and looked at it, surprised.

Applause broke out suddenly as the others grinned at him.

William smiled as he handed the cup to the keg guy and asked, "Can I have another?"

While his cup was being filled, the others began to talk among themselves again, ignoring him. Taking advantage of the fact that he was being ignored, William turned his back to them, pulled his chart from his pocket and unfolded it. He glanced over it frantically and shook his head.

"Whoa," he muttered. "This is gonna be harder to follow than I *thought.*"

"You want your beer, or *what?*" the keg guy called.

William wadded the chart up and stuffed it into his pocket quickly as he turned around, smiling. "Oh, yeah, you bet. Hand it over . . . *dude.*"

The keg guy smirked as he handed the beer over. "You know, there's something wrong with you," he said. "But I think you got some hope."

"Thanks," William said as he began to drain his second cup of beer.

Amanda and her friends had gathered in the fancy room that had been closed off by a tape barrier earlier in the evening. The tape was currently on the floor . . . again. Amanda was reclining on an antique chaise lounge. Cindi and Debi were sitting around her, Indian-style, on the floor, while Beth sat on the edge of the chaise at her feet.

"Seriously, guys," Amanda said, "I'm over it. *Really.*"

Cindi made a scoffing sound, and the other two shook their heads.

"*What?*" Amanda asked. "What is the *problem?*"

"Nothing," Beth said. "It's just . . . well, he *is* the most *dope* guy in school, y'know?"

"Yeah," Amanda said, nodding. "And school's *over.*"

Beth, Cindi, and Debi exchanged confused glances, as if Amanda had suddenly spoken in a foreign tongue. Hindustani, maybe.

"Who does he think he *is,* anyway," Cindi asked, "Brad Pitt?"

"Yeah, exactly!" Debi agreed. "And you're, like . . . *Gwyneth!*"

"Seriously!" Beth chimed in. "But Amanda, you *know* Brad regrets breaking up with her!"

Amanda gave them a forced smile. She wasn't sure how much more of their sympathy she could take.

"That's really sweet of you guys," she said, "but I really—"

"No, we *mean* it!" Debi cried. "You are *so* Gwyneth!"

"*Totally* Gwyneth," Cindi added. "But prettier!"

"Totally prettier," Beth said. "With bigger boobs!"

"Totally bigger boobs!" Debi shouted.

Amanda felt as if she were being smothered by an Oprah audience. She sat up on the edge of the chaise and said, "You know, I think I might need to get some air."

"Well, he's sure no Brad!" Cindi said, as if Amanda hadn't spoken.

"He's not even Brad in *Twelve Monkeys,*" Debi said, "all crazy and dirty and with that weird eye."

Cindi's eyes widened, as if she'd been insulted. "Mike Dexter doesn't even deserve to share *airspace* with Brad!"

Debi declared, "Mike Dexter is an *asshole!*"

All three girls cheered and got up on their knees to hug Amanda.

She wriggled out of their multiple embraces and stood. "Look, I don't want to talk about this, okay? I just . . . don't want . . . to *talk* about it!" She walked away from them.

Once Amanda was across the room and nearing the doorway, Beth whispered, "I don't think she's prettier than Gwyneth."

"Amanda, wait!" Cindi cried.

Preston had followed Amanda to the once tape-barriered room, and he'd been standing just outside the doorway, right next to a large fern, ever since she'd entered. Listening. Every now and then, he'd peeked around the edge of the doorway, *very* careful not to be seen.

He was amazed, absolutely amazed. She was *not*

broken up over the fact that Mike Dexter had dumped her! That meant he still had a chance!

Amanda suddenly walked out of the room.

Preston spun around and stepped face-first into the fern, hoping Amanda hadn't noticed him standing there at the doorway eavesdropping on her and her friends. He waited a long moment, then turned and started to follow Amanda . . . and collided with her friends as they hurried after her.

"Watch it!" Cindi barked.

"What are you *doing?*" Debi snapped.

"You freak!" Beth added.

The three of them hurried away, hot on Amanda's tail.

Preston smiled. It was okay. He didn't mind that they'd insulted him. Because . . . there was *hope!*

Chapter 10

*H*OPE.

Kenny spotted the next girl on his list, Ashley Fuller, a raven-haired beauty. She was heading in Kenny's direction, and he intercepted her on the way into the living room.

"Yo, Ashley," he said. "Myyyy-oh-*my,* you be lookin' fine to*night.*"

She gave him a detached glance and muttered, "Oh, thanks." Then she started to step around him.

Kenny was too quick for her, though, and stayed in front of her. "Check dis," he said, "I was reminiscin' today. And I was thinkin' 'bout dat time at Lynn Eckert's party in seventh grade. 'Member dat? We were all playin' Spin da Bottle?"

"Uh . . . I guess so," she said uncertainly, frowning.

"You and me, we never *did* get to kiss. But I hadda

mad flash of you starin' at me that night, just starin' at me all night long. Right? You 'member that? Kinda gigglin' a little wit' your girlfriends?"

Ashley looked confused for a moment, then her face brightened and she smiled.

Yes! Kenny thought, grinning. *It's working!*

"Oh, yeah," Ashley said, pointing at him. "I *do* remember!"

"Yeah, see? I knew you would." Kenny began to laugh.

"You were eating Chee•tos, and all that"—Ashley made an unpleasant face and waggled her fingers in front of her mouth—"all that *orange* stuff was stuck in your braces." She began nodding as she remembered more clearly. "Yeah, that's right, and no one wanted to tell you about it, so you just kept eating them and eating them and—God, Lynn and I thought that was the *funniest!*"

Kenny swallowed his laughter and his smile fell away. "Uh, well, uh . . . dass not how *I* be rememberin' it."

Ashley waved her arm at someone behind Kenny and shouted, "Lynn! C'mere!"

Lynn Eckert joined them. She was a perky blonde with a loud, high laugh.

"I'm telling Kenny about how we used to call him Chester Cheetah," Ashley said, giggling.

"Oh, yeah!" Lynn exclaimed, turning to Kenny. "Because of all that orange stuff in your braces at my party in seventh grade!" Lynn threw back her head and released a long stream of shrill, high-pitched laughter.

Olaf Van Hermert wandered by, and when he saw Ashley and Lynn laughing so hard, he stopped and stepped between them. He looked at Kenny and began laughing with the girls.

"Hey," Kenny snapped at the foreigner. "What're *you* laughin' at?" He backed up a few steps, then turned and hurried around the corner and down the hall. Above all the sounds in the house, he could still hear Lynn Eckert's piercing laughter.

Kenny sighed as he took out his notebook and pencil, glanced around to make sure no one was watching, then opened the notebook. He crossed Ashley's name off the list.

"Okay, not a problem," he muttered as he returned the notebook and pencil to his pocket.

He went into the kitchen, stood in line for a couple minutes to get a beer, then headed for the dining room. He glanced to his left and stopped. Sitting at the small table in the breakfast room was Stephanie Camber. She was a beautiful cheerleader with hair the color of honey, big blue eyes, and full pouty lips; and she was on his list.

Kenny sauntered over to the table, put a foot up on a chair, and leaned an elbow on his knee. He smiled and said, "Hey, Stephanie."

She was staring blankly out at the crowd in the dining room.

Kenny thought maybe she hadn't heard him, so he raised his voice and said, "Hey, 'sup, Stephanie?"

Stephanie didn't look at him, didn't even blink. She just kept staring.

Kenny decided to try a different approach.

"Damn, it is *noisy* in here," he said. "Wanna go talk outside? Should be quieter out there."

Without looking at Kenny or moving, Stephanie said in a monotone voice, "Okay."

Kenny moved away from the chair and stepped in front of her, hoping to get her attention. "Do you, uh . . . want a drink?" he asked.

"Okay," she said again, still unmoving, voice still flat, almost robotic.

Kenny leaned down and waved a hand in front of Stephanie's face. She didn't react at all, didn't even blink. He couldn't tell if she was staring at the crowd in the dining room, or at something on the other side of the universe.

"Uh . . . how 'bout if I poison it?" Kenny asked.

"Okay," she repeated in exactly the same way.

Kenny stood up straight and smiled. Stephanie Camber was *gone*. The light was off, nobody was home, and the attic had been cleaned *out*. He didn't know what kind of substance she'd consumed, or how much, but it was enough to send her on a five-year mission with the Starship *Enterprise*.

This is it, he thought. *This is my chance!*

Kenny stepped closer to her and said, "Hey, whaddaya say we, uh . . . y'know, go upstairs and—"

"Stephanie!" a girl screamed behind him.

Kenny spun around so quickly, he nearly fell over.

Candy Salter, a petite girl with short brown hair, rushed to Stephanie's side and put an arm around her.

"Thank *God* you found her!" Candy said to

Kenny. "She took three thingies of herbal ecstasy and wandered off! She's so out of it, *anything* could have happened and she probably wouldn't even *remember!* God, I was so worried somebody was . . . well, y'know, taking *advantage* of her, or something!" Candy helped Stephanie to her feet, put an arm around her, and led her out of the breakfast room, saying, "C'mon, honey, I'm gonna take you to the car."

"Okay," Stephanie said one last time.

Kenny sighed and shook his head. He'd been so close! He drained his beer, squashed the cup in his fist, and tossed it into an overflowing trash can. He removed the notebook and pencil from his pocket, crossed Stephanie's name off the list, then replaced the notebook and pencil in one smooth, practiced movement. With another sigh, he passed through the kitchen and entered the dining room.

He moved to the beat of the music as he passed through the crowd, trying to make himself feel better, trying to lift his own spirits. Then he froze.

Just a few feet away from him stood Jana Newton, talking with some girls. Jana was a tall redhead, and probably the most gorgeous girl on his rapidly shortening list.

Okay, now, he thought, *you da man . . . you da man.*

Kenny approached Jana and stood beside her for a moment, waiting for her to notice him. She went on talking to her friends for a moment, as if he weren't there. Then she glanced at him and flashed him a large but stiff smile, then continued talking.

Kenny inched closer to her and said, "Yo, Jana, wanna dance?"

"Sorry, I'm allergic," she said, glancing at him again. Without missing a beat, she continued her conversation.

"Uh . . . you're allergic? To *dancin'*?"

"Yeah," she said.

A moment later, Jana and her friends walked away, leaving Kenny standing alone. With another in a long series of sighs, Kenny pulled out his notebook and crossed Jana's name off his list as he wandered through the crowd.

As Kenny slipped his notebook back into his pocket, he passed William Lichter, who was walking in the opposite direction . . . but not too steadily. William pulled his folded up chart from his pocket and tried to unfold it. The sheet of paper seemed to resist his efforts, and William began to get frustrated. He bumped into people as he stumbled along, but he'd stopped saying "Excuse me" quite a while ago. No one noticed.

William was beginning to wonder if perhaps he'd had a bit too much to drink. Never having drunk alcohol before, he wasn't sure how much was too much. Fortunately, he still had his blood-alcohol level chart. He finally got the sheet of paper unfolded and stopped walking to study it.

"Wait a second," William mumbled to himself. "This isn't my chart. Uh . . . is it?"

All the lines on the page were blurred and runny, as if the page had gotten wet. But it was perfectly dry. He turned it sideways, then upside down.

William squinted his eyes at the page, and for just a moment, the chart cleared up enough for him to almost make it out. He realized it was his vision that was out of focus, not the page itself.

Did that mean he was drunk? But he didn't *feel* drunk. He felt fine. He realized, grinning, that he actually felt *great!*

"More beer comin' through!" someone shouted.

The crowd parted and William watched three guys roll a new keg toward the kitchen.

"More beer?" William muttered. Then he called, "Hey! Where y'goin' with that?" William hurried after the keg, grinning as he bounced off other partyers like a pinball.

Chapter 11

AMANDA HAD MANAGED TO LOSE HER THREE GIRL-friends and was wandering through the foyer alone. Beth, Cindi, and Debi were good friends, but they tended to overdo things a little, especially sympathy. Amanda did not need sympathy from them or anyone else. What she wanted more than anything in the world was to stop talking about the fact that Mike Dexter had broken up with her.

She was about to go into the living room when she heard someone say her name. She stopped, looked around, but saw no one. It had come from around the corner, down the hall. Two familiar voices were talking about her as they drew closer. Amanda recognized them immediately: Lynda Connely and Madison Sharpe, the biggest gossips at Huntington High. Amanda stepped over to the corner and waited out of their sight at the end of the hall as Lynda and Madison headed toward her.

"I heard Mike broke up with Amanda *last year,*" Lynda said.

"Last year?" Madison gasped. "But nobody said a word! I didn't hear a thing about it!"

"And do you know why?" Lynda continued. "I heard Amanda was paying him fifty bucks a month just to *act* like they were still together!"

"What?"

"Yes! Can you believe it? I thought—"

Amanda stepped in front of them when they reached the foyer.

Lynda and Madison froze, mouths still open.

Amanda did not speak. She simply gave them a look. It was a look that said that was the *stupidest* thing she'd ever heard in her life. Then she walked away.

"Jeez, what's with *her?*" Lynda asked as Amanda left the foyer.

With a giggle, Madison replied, "Not Mike Dexter anymore!"

Both girls squealed with laughter.

Preston made his way through the crowd in the den, a beer in hand. He kept scanning the room, looking for Amanda. The right moment hadn't come along yet, that was all. When it came time to give Amanda his letter, when the time was really *right,* he would know it. He would *feel* it.

"Preston!" someone shouted behind him.

Preston turned to face Woody Cusack, a thin guy of average height with wire-rimmed glasses. He remembered Woody from gym class: He was not especially good at anything, but incredibly enthusiastic about *everything*.

"Hi, Woody."

"Aww, Preston, man, I'm so glad I got to see you! I know you're leaving tomorrow and like—" He smacked himself on the forehead with the palm of his hand. *"Man!* I'm *totally* gonna *miss* you!"

Preston smiled. "Well, gee, Woody, thanks." He turned and started walking again, heading for the living room.

"Like, I was *totally* remembering that time in seventh grade," Woody said, falling into step beside Preston, "when we mashed up *all* the food on our lunch trays and you paid me a dollar to eat it? And I did? Remember that? That was the *best!"*

Oh, great, Preston thought. *I don't need this now.* But he smiled again and nodded, saying, "Oh, yeah, yeah. We had some good times, huh?" He picked up his pace then, trying to lose Woody on the way to the living room.

"And how about during softball when Ricky Feldman hit that line drive," Woody went on, keeping up with Preston, "and it hit you right in the *nuts?"* He laughed loudly. "Man, that was the *funniest!"*

Preston decided to try ignoring him. He entered the living room and went on doing what he'd been doing all evening: looking for Amanda.

He stumbled to a halt when he saw her. She was standing at the snack table putting a few potato

76

chips on a small paper plate. Others watched her, but no one was talking to her. She was *alone.*

This is it, Preston thought. *This is the moment!*

He pressed between the bodies, making his way to the table. He vaguely heard Woody behind him, going on and on about his favorite moments during their school years together, but Preston paid him no attention. He was too busy taking a few deep breaths, steeling himself for his encounter with Amanda.

Preston stopped at the table and faced her. She stood directly across from him, scooping some dip onto her plate. He did not take his eyes from her for a moment, but she didn't notice him as she put a few celery sticks on her plate. Preston opened his mouth to say her name, to get her attention, but nothing came out. He tried again.

"Am . . ." It was the best he could do, but it worked, because she looked up.

She looked at *him!* Amanda looked directly into his eyes! She looked curious, a little confused, but she was waiting. It was *obvious* she was waiting for him to continue to talk to her!

"Am . . . Ama . . ." It wasn't working. He couldn't get her name out of his mouth, and she was watching him with slightly narrowed eyes and just a hint of a smirk, as if she might think—oh, God, as if she might think he was trying to be *funny!* He decided to skip the small talk.

Preston reached for the letter in his back pocket. *I'll just give it to her and let it speak for itself . . . and for me, as well.*

"And how about that time when we went on the field trip to the meat packing plant and you threw up in your bookbag?" Woody came to Preston's side. "That was the *funniest!*"

Amanda looked at Woody.

Preston looked at Woody. "That wasn't *me!*" Preston snapped, pulling his hand out of his pocket.

"Sure it was! Remember? 'Cause you tried to leave the bag behind on the bus so no one would see it, but Vice Principal Biller brought it around to all the classes trying to find out whose it was! Remember?"

Mortified, Preston turned to Amanda. She was looking at him again. She looked . . . *embarrassed* for him. She averted her eyes and grabbed a few olives, then turned and walked away from the table, looking as if she couldn't figure out what else to do.

Preston's heart dropped from his chest, down through his abdomen, past his hip, all the way down his leg, and landed like a rock in his left foot. He turned slowly and faced Woody, teeth clenched.

"And I was, like, 'Hey, Preston!'" Woody continued, smiling as if nothing had happened. "I said, 'Hey, isn't that *your* bag?'" he said, laughing. "Remember? And you were, like—"

Preston spun away from Woody and strode across the room. He was angry at Woody . . . and humiliated.

Woody followed him. "Hey, Preston, remember that time in the locker room when you—"

Preston turned on him, lips curled back over his teeth in an angry smile. "Hey, Woody!" he shouted.

Does Preston have a chance with Amanda, now that Mike has dumped her?

Amanda Beckett

Preston Meyers

Mike Dexter

Kenneth Fisher

Denise Fleming

William Lichter

The Party!

Kenny practices his "technique."

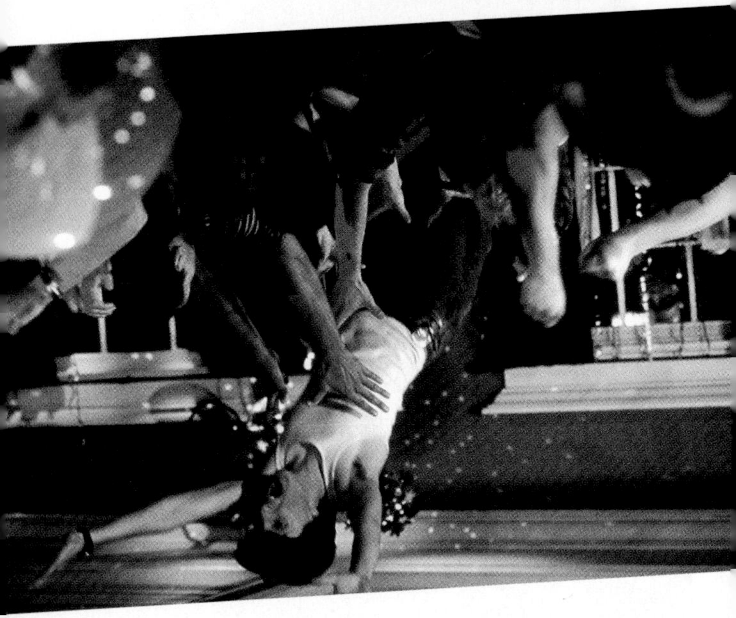

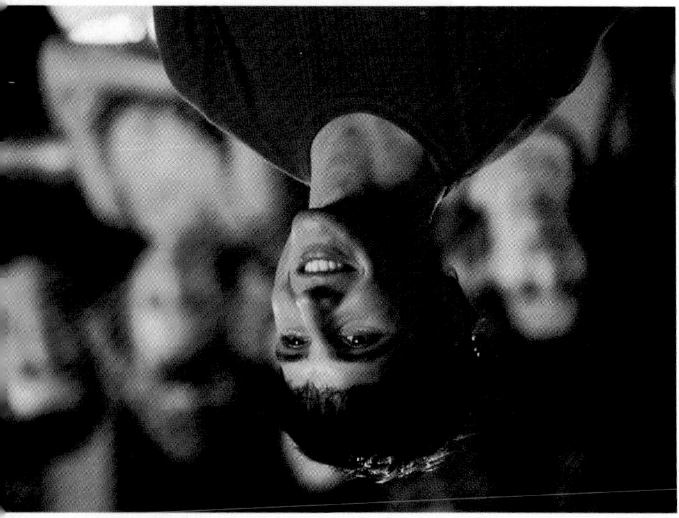

Amanda searches
for Preston after
reading his letter.

Meanwhile,
Preston is talking
to Angel.

A happy ending for Preston and Amanda?

Woody flinched and his mouth shut so abruptly, his teeth clicked together.

"I've got one!" Preston said. "Remember that time when I was about to talk to this girl, and you came up and started telling all those completely *asinine* stories?"

Woody frowned slightly, thinking about it. "No, I don't remember that."

"Well, *that's* funny!" Preston shouted. "Because it was only about five *seconds* ago!"

Preston turned and hurried away, and this time, Woody didn't follow him. Instead, Woody lifted a fist in the air and called out, "And I won't forget it, guy! Good times, man, we've had some *good times!"*

"What a *dork!"* Preston hissed as he left the living room, embarrassed and defeated, but still not without hope.

As Amanda walked away from the snack table, she was approached by her cousin Ron. She smiled when she saw him coming, but she really hoped he didn't want to talk. That was what Ron did best . . . talking. He thought everything could be solved by talking it out. They were second cousins by marriage, but he was fond of bringing up their family ties.

He ambled over to her. Ron was tall, with a mouth a little too big for his face, an Adam's apple a little too big for his neck, wearing his usual khakis. Ron always wore khakis.

"Amanda, hey," he said, stepping very close to

her. He draped an arm around her shoulders and leaned close to her ear. "I just heard you and Mike broke up."

"Hi, Ron," Amanda said.

"Well, I just can't believe you didn't *tell* me," he said. "I mean, we're *family.*"

Amanda closed her eyes before rolling them, just to be polite. "We're second cousins, Ron."

"Exactly," he said, nodding as he gave her a squeeze. "We should be able to talk about these things. In fact, I think we *should* talk. Let's go someplace a little more quiet, okay?"

Amanda really didn't *want* to, but so far, the party wasn't much fun at all, what with everyone going on and on about Mike. She decided it was better than nothing and left the living room with her cousin Ron.

In the kitchen, Kenny stood by the trash can— which was now buried under a pile of trash— looking at his list with despair. Each of the ten names had a line drawn through it. He'd run out of babes, and it wasn't even late yet.

"Yo, *cheeze!*" Sammy shouted as he and Richie walked into the kitchen. "Whassup?"

Kenny shoved the notebook into his pocket and smiled at his homeys.

"Yeah," Richie said, "shouldn't you be gettin' your freak on now?"

"Yo, man," Kenny said. "I'm juss hangin' while dose two over dere scratch it out over who gets t'knock boots wit' me."

Sammy and Richie looked around the kitchen, then looked through the doorway into the dining room, then over the bar into the living room.

"What two?" Sammy asked.

"I don' see no two," Richie said.

"Yo," Kenny said defensively, giving Sammy a firm shove. "You callin' me a *liar?"*

Sammy's smile disappeared and he scowled at Kenny, shoving him back. "Who you *shovin',* brother?"

Kenny shook his head and turned away from them, backing down. He was too depressed to deal with it at the moment.

"Damn," he said as he walked away, "why you gotta waste my flava?"

He crossed the kitchen and squeezed through the doorway, where Jake Wickley had his girlfriend, Beth, pressed against the doorjamb, their mouths locked together. Once he got by them, he turned left in the hall and headed for the foyer, passing Mike Dexter, who was going in the opposite direction.

Mike stopped outside the kitchen and stared at Jake for a long moment. He couldn't believe it. They were supposed to be breaking up with their girl-friends, and there was Jake, giving Beth mouth-to-mouth in the kitchen doorway. He reached out and tapped Jake's shoulder. No reaction. He *slapped* Jake's shoulder and said, "Hey, dude. Can I talk to you?"

Jake was startled and pulled away from Beth so suddenly, their mouths made a sucking-popping sound. "Yeah?"

"C'mere," Mike said, grabbing his elbow. He led Jake a few steps down the hall, where a line was beginning to form outside the bathroom. "What's goin' on, man? Did you do it?"

"Do what?" Jake asked.

"Break *up* with her!"

"Oh, yeah, I'm . . . I'm workin' on it, man."

"Workin' on it?" Mike asked with a chuckle. "Dude, you were just licking her *lungs!"*

"Well, yeah, I know, but I'm gonna do it. I'm workin' *up* to it."

"Then hurry up! I just saw a whole Jeep full of hot chicks pull up outside! They're from another school, dude, and they'd be all *over* us in two *seconds,* if you'd just drop the excess baggage you're carryin' around, man. You understand?"

"Yeah, well, I don't know, Mike."

"You don't *know?"*

"Hey, listen, man, Beth's parents are away and she was kinda thinkin' we could stay at her place tonight, and . . . y'know . . ."

"But what about the plan?" Mike asked emphatically. "What about the *pact?"*

"I know, I know, but . . ." Jake sighed and his head wagged from side to side for a moment. "See, her parents got a *mirror* over their bed!"

Mike took a step backward, shaking his head. "Okay. Okay, man, that's fine. Tell you what. I'll go see what the other guys are up to. Maybe *they've* got some balls."

Mike turned away and stalked back up the hall toward the foyer. Jake watched him leave, then returned to the kitchen doorway, where Beth was still leaning against the doorjamb, waiting for him. Their mouths were pressed together again in less than a second.

Mike walked into the den, looking for Ben and T.J. He went through the whole room, asking a few people if they'd seen his friends. Finally, he gave up and decided to try another part of the house. On his way out of the den, he passed a sofa, where Denise Fleming was sitting alone, slumped low.

Denise had a large ceramic bowl of M&M's in her lap. She was sifting through them, looking for the blue ones. Whenever she found a blue one, she ate it. There was a guy sitting by the fireplace with a guitar singing Broadway show tunes, which clashed with the music thundering from the living room. He didn't seem to mind, though, as he made his way through "Cabaret."

No one wanted to talk to her. She'd tried to start a conversation or two on her way into the den, but without success. Denise kept telling herself she didn't mind, that it really didn't matter, because she'd only come to this stupid party as a favor to Preston in the first place. But it did matter, in a way, because . . . well, because she was *there!* Everyone was talking to each *other,* but not to her. And besides, if she couldn't get anyone to *talk* to her, how was she going to get anyone to drive her *home?*

She found another blue M&M and popped it into her mouth, enjoying the feeling of it being crushed between her molars.

Denise was surprised when a girl came over to the

sofa and cautiously sat down beside her. She'd seen the girl around before, recognized her face, but didn't know the girl's name. The girl looked at Denise as if she were about to speak, but she seemed shy. Denise sat up straight and smiled at the girl.

"Hi," the girl said.

"Hi," Denise replied. She held out the bowl and said, "Want some M&M's?"

"No, thanks."

Denise put the bowl back in her lap.

The girl said, "Hey, weren't you in my language lab?"

Denise brightened. "Yes! I knew you from *somewhere,* I just couldn't remember where. Yes, we were in language lab together."

The girl jumped off the sofa and rushed over to three other girls, laughing. "Ha!" she crowed. "See? I *told* you she went to our school! Now, pay up!"

The four girls left the den as three of them handed money to the girl who had been sitting with Denise.

With a long sigh, Denise slumped back down in the sofa. She felt a pang in her chest as she ate another blue M&M.

The band was ready to play. Walter had gone to the kitchen to get a glass of water, but Jimmy, Dan, and Brian were ready and waiting.

Walter hurried through the crowded dining room, then through the crowd in the living room, and finally made it to the cleared-out end of the room where the band was set up. He took a sip of the water, set it on the amp, lit a cigarette, and nodded once at the band. Taking the mike from its stand, he said, "Okay, one, two—" He froze and stared at the floor for a moment, then replaced the microphone on its stand and turned to the band. "What're you doin'?" he asked Jimmy.

"Wearin' one of our T-shirts. You know, for the publicity."

"No, no, no," Walter said, shaking his head. "Those are for the fans! The *band* doesn't wear its own T-shirts!"

"Hey," Brian said. "I think it's cool." He turned around and removed a T-shirt from the enormous pile in the corner.

"Oh, jeez," Walter groaned, rubbing his eyes with thumb and forefinger.

"Well, if they get to wear the shirts," Dan said, "I wanna wear my hat." He ducked down to reach behind the drums. When he sat up again, he was wearing a cowboy hat. A *huge* cowboy hat.

"What the hell is *that?*" Walter asked.

"This is my hat."

"*Your* hat? That's enough hat for about *five* people!"

"Well, this is my hat," Dan said, "and I'm stickin' with it."

"Oh, God," Walter said, hanging his head, "we are *so* doomed." He threw his cigarette aside hard, frustrated and angry.

The cigarette butt landed just beneath the drapes that were open on the window that looked out over the back patio. It didn't take long for the glowing ember at the end of that cigarette butt to ignite a flame at the bottom of that drape.

"Oh, my God!" Molly Stinson cried when she saw the flames. She ran to the drapes and began stomping on the small fire. It was out in seconds, but her parents' drapes suddenly had a hem of scorched blackness. "Oh, God . . . oh . . . *God!*" she said to herself as she hunkered down and looked at the burned edge. "They're gonna *kill* me! They're gonna—" She spotted the cigarette butt and the blackened hole it had made in the carpet. She picked up the butt, stood, turned to face the crowd, and opened her mouth to shout at them about it, to chew them out for their carelessness and lack of consideration, but something made her stop.

It was a smell. An *odor.* Her nose wrinkled as she sniffed the air a few times.

"Do I smell *poop?*" she asked loudly. "I smell poop! Does someone have poop on their shoe? On my parents' *carpet?*"

No one paid any attention to her.

"God*dammit!*" Molly shouted. She dropped the cigarette butt, got down on her hands and knees, and began crawling around on the floor, smelling everyone's feet.

Two of the feet she smelled belonged to Kenny Fisher, who was slumped dejectedly in an overstuffed recliner. He was depressed because he'd reached the end of his list of girls, and he was still alone. "Alone" seemed to be an incurable condition for him that night. He let Molly Stinson lift his feet and sniff them, then watched her crawl away to sniff others, shaking his head at whatever pathetic thing she was into.

Kenny slumped down even farther in his chair, hoping Sammy and Richie wouldn't find him.

He heard a girl crying behind him; sniffling and sobbing and crying.

"And . . . and then I heard he slept with some . . . some . . . suh-suh-*sophomore!*" the girl wailed.

"That *pig!*" another girl said. "What are you gonna do?"

Kenny listened as the first girl began to compose herself. There was a lot of sniffling, some nose-blowing, a few coughs. Finally, she spoke: "I'm going to beat him at his own game. I'm gonna have sex with someone tonight . . . at this party. And I'm gonna make make sure Jason finds out!"

"Right *on!*" the other girl said. "Empower yourself, girl. But wait. With *who?*"

"Who cares?" the first girl asked. "The . . . the next guy who hits on me." She laughed bitterly. "Oh, hell, the first guy who *talks* to me!"

Upon hearing this, Kenny's entire body stiffened. The recliner reclined, and then fell over backward.

Kenny found himself look up at two lovely girls, and he realized how foolish he must look to them. He was on his feet in seconds, brushing himself off and smiling at the girls. One was blond, the other was brunette. It was the brunette whose eyes were puffy from crying.

She was beautiful—*gorgeous*—the kind of girl any guy would *kill* for . . . and she was ready to have sex with the first guy who *talked* to her just to get back at her boyfriend.

Kenny stepped up to her and said, "Well, I must've died and gone to heaven, 'cause I got an angel standin' right in front of me. Y'know, you should be—" He stopped and pretended to notice her tears for the first time. "Are you *crying?*" He stepped back and stomped a foot. "Aw, *no!* Sweetheart, you are *far* too fine to look so sad!"

She sniffled. "Yeah, sure."

"Aw, now, don't be dat way," he said, frowning. "C'mon, it breaks my heart to see you like this. You tell me what Special K can do to make you feel better."

She looked at her blond friend, who shrugged, as if to say, *He'll do.* She looked at Kenny again, gulped, and said, "Okay, come out to the poolhouse with me."

Kenny smiled. He stood there smiling for a long moment, thinking about his backpack, his Love Kit. There was *no way* he could go to the poolhouse without a quick visit to the bathroom. He had to make sure everything he needed was handy, had to sort all his stuff out. Everything had to be right!

"Okay," he said finally, nodding. "I just need to . . . I kind of have to . . . could you just, um . . . wait here? For one minute? Just one minute! And I promise, I'll be right back." He hurried away, stopped, went back, and said, "Don't move. Please, I mean . . . *please* . . . do *not* move!" He hurried away again, and this time, he didn't stop until he was in the foyer.

His heart was pounding, his mouth was dry, and he had the strange feeling that his hair hurt.

"Ah-right," he muttered to himself as he headed for the hall. "Bathroom, pee, underarm check. Breath Assure, you just hold up, okay? Just hold up. Lessee, do I put da jimmy hat on *now,* in case she—" He stopped when he saw the line outside the bathroom. It was a long line. A *very* long line. And at the head of the line, the bathroom door was open . . . and a guy on crutches was slowly, clumsily making his way in.

"Oh, God," Kenny said as he took his place at the end of the line.

He was in for a wait, and so was the girl who was waiting for him.

Chapter 12

GEOFF PICCIRILLI AND MURPHY PELAN WERE WAITing, lying on the roof of the poolhouse, gazing at the stars overhead as the party picked up below.

"I think I just saw something," Geoff whispered. He sat up next to Murphy, as if a change of position might give him a better view of the night sky.

"You did not," Murphy said. He didn't move.

"I *swear*. It was like a blue streak. It just whizzed by! I'm *telling* you, Murphy, that patch of sky right over those power lines is like a superhighway of UFO activity!"

"I've never seen anything fly over those power lines," Murphy said.

"Because you don't pay attention, Murphy. How many times do I have to tell you—you've gotta pay *attention*."

"I'm too bored to pay attention right now. How long have we been up here, anyway, Geoff?"

Geoff laid back down with a sigh. "Too long. I wonder how William's doing. I hope he's not having any trouble blending in."

William was blending quite well in the breakfast room with half a dozen other kids he'd never spoken to before in his life. Everyone in the breakfast room had had more than his share of beer—the room *reeked* of it—and all the guys were lined up, beers in hand, watching William. As William sprinkled salt on the lovely neck of a girl named Rochelle, the guys chanted, "Bill! Bill! Bill! Bill!"

William looked up from Rochelle's neck suddenly and blinked several times. He was suddenly overcome by the nagging feeling that he'd forgotten something, or lost something, or was missing something. It was a strong feeling, but he just couldn't put his finger on the source of it.

"Wasn't there something I was supposed to do tonight?" he muttered to himself.

"Whadja say, Billy?" Rochelle asked.

He frowned, thought about it a moment longer, then shook his head and smiled. "Nothin'."

William licked the salt off Rochelle's neck, then two other girls stepped up to him from each side. Wendy handed him a shot of tequila, which he downed immediately. He leaned over to Brenda, who held a lime wedge between her teeth. William put his mouth to hers, plucked the wedge from her and sucked on it. He took the lime wedge from his mouth and tossed it over his shoulder as he let out a long, loud, *"Woo-hoooo!"* and the others in the room cheered him raucously.

Suddenly, William's knees weakened and he began to wobble, as if he were standing on a waterbed.

"I can't feel my legs!" William shouted through a grin. "I have no legs!"

The others cheered again, then downed their beers.

"You know, Amanda," Ron said, "I know we're not all that close, but . . . you could've called me. I happen to be a great listener."

Amanda was seated on a small sofa next to her cousin in the room that had once been closed off by a tape barrier. As Ron talked, he ate potato chips from her plate.

"Thanks, Ron," she said. "It's just . . . well, I mean, it all *just* happened, so I'm still trying to sort it all out, you know?"

"Sure," he replied, nodding. He leaned a little closer to her and said confidentially, "But if you ask me, I never really saw you two together in the first place."

"Yeah," Amanda said with a cold chuckle. "You and me both."

"What?"

She sighed. "Well, I mean, I know why I *started* dating him. I just don't know why I did it for so *long.*"

Ron narrowed his eyes and said, "Um, you're

gonna have to explain that one to me." Then he dipped another chip and plopped it into his mouth.

"It's just that, at first," Amanda explained, "it was all so unbelievable, you know? At my old junior high I was always just this little . . . *nobody.* Then I came to Huntington freshman year and Mike Dexter wanted to *date* me, and I was, like, suddenly Miss Popular! I . . . I know it's really lame, but . . . well, it felt good. It was the first time I ever felt cool in my life." She rolled her eyes and released a single, breathy laugh. "Puh-*leeze*—it was the first time I ever had a *boyfriend.*"

"So, what happened?" Ron asked.

"Nothing. And that's the problem." She realized she wasn't hungry anymore and handed the plate with its remaining snacks over to Ron, then leaned back on the sofa. "I mean, Mike's still the same person *now* that he was then. Mooning the guy at the drive-through window, giving the underclassmen wedgies . . ."

Ron winced at that and nodded. "Yeah, uh . . . I've, um, heard he does that." He shifted uncomfortably on the sofa, as if experiencing an unpleasant memory. "So, why didn't you just break up with him?"

"I was . . . scared. Of being alone." She frowned as she chewed thoughtfully on her lower lip. "You know, we were together for four years. That's . . . *forever.* So who am I if I'm not Mike's *girlfriend?* No one knows me as anything else." She leaned back her head and looked up at the ceiling. "I don't think *I* know me as anything else," she added, sounding upset with herself.

"Well, *I* know you," Ron said, scooting a little closer to Amanda. "And I think you're a *really* great person."

Amanda lifted her head and gave her cousin a little smile. "You *have* to say that. We're related."

"Only by marriage," he said with a grin.

"Look, I don't know about you," Preston said, "but I really believe there's gotta be one person out there who's . . . you know, *the one*. I know that's not an earth-shattering new theory, or anything, but . . . if you think about it, it's really stunning. Just . . . *one* . . . person."

He was sitting on the concrete beside the pool, watching the fragments of light shimmer over the surface of the water. Next to him sat a guy he didn't even know. But Preston had had a couple beers and he was feeling talkative, so he was spilling his guts.

"My one person," Preston continued, "has gotta be Amanda. I mean, look at everything that's been building for the past four years. All that stuff *had* to have happened for a reason." He took the letter from his back pocket and held it up. "And that's what *this* is. It's not just some sappy love letter telling her how my heart stops every time I see her, or that her smile ranks up there as one of the most beautiful things in the world. Although it *does* say that. And it's not just to tell her she's so much more than homecoming queen, or Mike Dexter's girlfriend, or how I know there's this *really* amazing person in there . . . a person no one's even bothering to see. Well, uh—" He shrugged. "All that's in there, too. But what it's *really* about is how, if she'd just give me a chance— one chance—maybe we could find out if there really is a reason for all of this. Why's she's not with Mike tonight and why, after four years, I'm still here with this letter." He chuckled. "And maybe we could find out what that reason is." He looked at the guy sitting next to him and said, "You know what? It's time to find out. I think I'm ready to do this. Finally." He stood and brushed off his jeans, then asked the guy, "Any words of encouragement?"

The foreigner grinned up at him and said, with a very thick accent, "Would you like to touch my penis?"

Preston's mouth dropped open in shock. "Uh . . . I-I-I . . . uh, right. I see." He started backing away, nodding. "I appreciate the, uh, the invitation and I'm, uh, flattered, but, uh . . . I think I should probably try and find Amanda again." He turned around and hurried away.

The exchange student stood quickly and called after him, "I am a sex machine!"

"Oh, jeez," Preston muttered as he headed into the house.

As Preston left, Mary Hampson wandered over to Olaf, the exchange student. She was still swaying drunkenly, and still crying. She said something to Olaf, but it was incomprehensibly lost in her sobs.[2]

---

[2]*"I'd* like to touch your penis!"

Inside the house, Mike Dexter stood with Ben Foss and T. J. Munson on the steps between the den and living room. Mike was shifting his weight from one foot to the other, back and forth, and he did *not* look happy.

"So, did you break up with 'em or not?" he asked the guys.

"We will, man, I promise!" Ben insisted. "It's just that . . . well, Cindi's dad got us all tickets to see Rage."

"What?" Mike snapped. "You mean, because of some stupid concert tickets—"

"No, wait, wait," Ben said, lifting his hands reassuringly. "We're gonna do it right after the concert, man, I *swear.*"

"Okay," Mike said, unconvinced. "When's the concert?"

Ben and T.J. exchanged a cautious glance, then T.J. said, "August."

Mike's eyes bulged. *"August?* Aw, jeez, you—you guys *suck!"* he said loudly.

"Hey, man," Ben said as he and T.J. began to back away from their angry buddy, "they're . . . y'know, they're really good seats."

"Later, dude," T.J. said.

The two of them turned and went back into the living room, where Cindi and Debi were waiting for them.

In the hallway, the line to get into the bathroom was growing.

"I can't believe this," Kenny Fisher mumbled to himself, buzzing with frustration.

The guy with the crutches, who'd been in the bathroom for what seemed like a month and a half, *finally* hobbled out and started making his way along the hall. The girl at the head of the line stepped into the bathroom and was about to close the door behind her.

"Jen!" another girl squealed from behind Kenny. "Wait for *us!*"

About a dozen girls ran along the line of waiting partyers and poured into the bathroom with the girl who'd just stepped inside. The door slammed shut behind them and a lock clicked.

"Dis be *suckin',*" Kenny grumbled, stepping out of the line and going back up the hall. There *had* to be at least one more bathroom in such a big house. He *hoped* there was, because he didn't want to waste any more time standing in line when he could be with that lovely girl out in the living room who was waiting for him to come help her make her boyfriend jealous.

Kenny hurried into the living room and looked around until he spotted the girl sitting on a love seat with her friend. She was still there, hadn't given up on him yet.

"Who did this?" a girl shrieked. "Who *did* this?"

Kenny turned toward the voice and saw Molly Stinson staring in horror at a large family portrait hanging on the wall. Someone had drawn nipples on her mother, and a thought bubble coming from her father's head contained the words I REALLY LIKE BOYS. He knew it was probably a bad time, but Kenny *had* to find another bathroom, and Molly was the one to ask.

"Um, look," he said approaching her cautiously, "is there another bathroom upstairs? Because the line down here's really long, and, uh, I really have to go."

Still staring at the violated portrait, Molly shook her head and said, "No one's allowed upstairs. Now, *who did this?*"

Kenny got a sudden idea. "You know, Molly," he said, "I thought I saw that foreign exchange student guy carrying a black Magic Marker." *Yes! That'll teach that dweeb to laugh at me.*

"Really?" she gasped, turning to face him. "Oh, that little foreign— All right," Molly said, after a moment's pause, "you can go upstairs. But *just* you!"

"Thanks!" Kenny exclaimed. He turned and bolted toward the foyer.

Molly called after him, "Hey, don't close the door all the way! It's kinda broken!" She turned to face the crowd in her living room, clenching her teeth angrily, and growled, "Okay, where *are* you, you Belgian freak?"

Denise Fleming glanced up at the portrait as Molly stormed by and held back a guilty chuckle, then continued looking at the books on the shelves in the living room. She walked slowly along the bookcases, head tilted sideways, reading the titles on the spines.

She hadn't asked anyone for a ride home because no one seemed to be leaving, and even if they were, most of them were so drunk or stoned, she'd rather walk home on her hands than get into a car with them. She hadn't seen Preston since he'd left her to go find Amanda. Denise was feeling bored . . . and a little lonely and sad.

Why couldn't she just cut loose and enjoy the party like everyone else? Why was she always so *serious?* Denise had never felt like other people her age, or any *other* age, for that matter. She just didn't *fit.* Never had. Coming to the graduation party had been a horrible idea and she was sorry she'd let Preston talk her into it.

Denise wandered over to the back door and stepped out onto the patio for a breath of night air. A group of kids were huddled together on the patio, heads leaning forward as they all stared intently at something. Curious, Denise walked over to see what was so interesting.

In the middle of the huddle stood William Lichter. He was holding a single leaf in his hand, and the others were staring at it in awe.

"Fifteen million cells," William said quietly. "Growing . . . dying . . . being reborn . . . a whole tiny universe . . . invisible to the naked eye."

"Ooooohhh, aaaaahhh," the group cooed in wonder.

They were all stoned out of the galaxy.

Denise went back inside and crossed the living room. She was stepping into the foyer when she heard Flower Kowalksi exclaim, "Dude! You're not supposed to put the weed *in* the brownie, you're supposed to melt it into the *butter!* This brownie is all wrong!"

Denise saw Flower standing with Eddie Wright in the foyer, saw her draw her arm back, saw her throw the brownie through the air, but Denise still didn't have time to duck. The brownie smacked into the side of her face and broke into a few gooey pieces, most of which stuck to her cheek and forehead.

She opened her eyes just in time to see Eddie hurrying out of the foyer after Flower, carrying a plate of brownies.

"But wait, baby!" he called. "We could still *smoke* this!"

Denise tried to wipe the chocolate goop from her face, but without success. She'd have to wash it off.

"Just when I thought the night couldn't get any more annoying," she said to herself with a sigh.

Preston still hadn't found Amanda, but he hadn't lost his courage.

In the dining room, a guy wearing a bright pink bikini bra on his head like a bonnet and carrying an armload of Reddi Wip cans passed by Preston. His name was Wilmer Beddoe.

"Hey, Wilmer," Preston said, putting a hand on the guy's shoulder. "Have you seen Amanda Beckett?"

"Uh, yeah," the guy said. "I just saw her a few minutes ago in that fancy room in the front, next to the foyer." He grinned. "Hey, didja hear that Mike

Dexter broke up with her this morning? I'm thinkin' about askin' her out."

Yeah, I'm sure she'd love your hat, Preston thought as he made his way through the crowd to find Amanda.

"Thanks for listening, Ron," Amanda said.

They were still sitting on the sofa. Ron had eaten all the chips and dip and had put the paper plate on an end table with only a few celery and carrot sticks remaining.

"I probably sound really whiny," Amanda continued. "I mean, I got to be Prom Queen. Poor me, huh? God, I should just shut up."

"No, no," Ron said reassuringly. "You need someone to listen . . . and I'm here for you." He moved closer to Amanda and stretched his arm on the back of the sofa behind her.

Amanda didn't notice. She was thinking, instead, of how tired she was and wondering if maybe she should just go home.

"You know, Amanda," Ron whispered, "I feel very . . . close to you right now."

Amanda detected something very odd in her cousin's voice and turned to look at him. He pounced the instant their eyes met, pressing his mouth to hers and kissing her passionately as he wrapped his arms around her and held her tightly.

At that moment, Preston came to the doorway of the room and saw Amanda locked in a kiss with some guy on the sofa. For a moment, Preston thought his heart had stopped beating. He couldn't breathe, couldn't move. . . . He could only stare. Only seconds passed, but it felt like an eternity before he finally turned and left the doorway.

What had appeared to be a passionate kiss to Preston was actually Amanda struggling to get out of her cousin's embrace. She finally pushed him away and shot to her feet, glaring down at him.

"Ron, what are you *doing?"* she cried, wiping her mouth with the back of her hand.

Ron reached up and pulled her back onto the sofa, wrapping his arms around her again as he tried to kiss her neck. "I care about you," he said, his voice muffled. "Really, Amanda, I want to—"

"Get *off* me!" she shouted, pushing him away again.

"C'mon, baby, it's okay. . . ." He tried to suck on her earlobe this time.

She pulled away from him. "You—you're *disgusting!"*

"Oh, c'mon, you were *begging* me to!" Ron insisted. " 'I need to be somebody's girlfriend,' you said—"

"That is *not* what I was saying!" Amanda stood again and wiped Ron's saliva from her neck and ear. "And besides, you—you're my *cousin!"*

"Through *marriage,"* Ron reminded her, standing.

She backed away from him. "Whatever. You're *sick."* She spun around angrily and stalked toward the doorway.

"Shit," Ron said. "Hey, Amanda, you're not gonna tell my parents about this, are you?"

Preston stood outside in the driveway, rereading his letter to Amanda in the glow of the porchlight.

He'd thought it was the moment. Everything had felt so *right*. But he'd hesitated, he'd waited too long. Instead of acting, he'd just moped around *thinking* about acting . . . and now it was too late. Amanda had already found someone else. Preston had lost her . . . again.

Molly hurried by him without even noticing he was there. She was carrying a huge, bulging garbage bag and talking to herself.

"These people are savages," she grumbled. "They're *animals!*" She took the bag over to a large garbage bin to the side of the driveway and stuffed it inside, then turned and headed back into the house, still complaining. "It's like inviting a National Geographic special over to the house, for crying out loud!" She slammed the door once she was inside.

Preston walked over to the garbage bin, stared at the letter for a moment longer, then tossed it into the bin with the rest of the trash. He walked down the driveway and headed for his car. He couldn't bear to go back inside.

As far as Preston was concerned, the party was over.

Chapter 13

IN THE UPSTAIRS BATHROOM, KENNY HAD HIS LOVE KIT open on the counter. He'd left the bathroom door open just a bit, as Molly had told him to, and went straight to work.

First, he checked under his arms. No problems there. His teeth were fine, but his breath could use a little work. He reached into his backpack for the Breath Assure, but instead, his copy of *The Kama Sutra* caught his attention. He removed the book and placed it on the counter. Kenny had marked several places in the book so he could refer easily to the illustrations of his favorite sexual positions. He opened it to one of those illustrations and began to read the text as he got the Breath Assure and poured several into the palm of his hand. Still reading, he tossed the little pills into his mouth, pulled a small paper cup from the dispenser on the wall, and filled it with water. His hand slowed to a stop as it lifted the cup to his mouth, and he frowned intently as he continued reading.

"Naw, man," he muttered, "dass impossible." His mouth was still full of Breath Assure and his words came out in a garbled jumble.

He looked at the illustration carefully, then slowly tried to copy the position held by the figure on the page. He lifted one leg, tried to lean backward, and promptly lost his balance. He landed on his back on the floor and spilled the cup of water on his pants. The pills were knocked back into his throat and he coughed and gagged as he scrambled to his feet, filled the cup with water again, and drank them all down.

Kenny took a few deep breaths to compose himself, then looked down at his pants. A large wet spot covered his fly and spread down between his legs.

"Aw, *man*," he groaned.

There was no *way* he could go back downstairs and meet that girl with a wet crotch. He had to work fast.

Kenny looked under the sink and found a blow-dryer. He plugged it in, pointed it at himself just below the waist and turned it on. The air from the dryer got hot fast. It got *very* hot *very* fast.

"Damn!" Kenny shouted, turning off the blow-dryer and putting it on the counter. "Damn, damn, *damn!*" He hopped around a little as he quickly removed his pants. "I wanna be hot," he muttered, "but I don' wanna be *dat* hot!"

He draped his pants over a chair and aimed the

blow-dryer at the wet spot with his left hand while reaching into his backpack with his right. He removed a strip of condoms and tried to remove a few individual packets from the strip with his teeth.

At that moment, as Kenny stood there in his underwear, blow-drying his water-stained pants, with a strip of condoms dangling from his mouth and an open copy of *The Kama Sutra* on the counter, Denise Fleming walked into the bathroom.

Kenny looked over at her and their eyes met. Both of them froze for a long moment, gawking at one another.

Denise screamed.

Kenny screamed. The condoms fell from his mouth as he dropped the blow-dryer and grabbed his pants.

Denise continued to scream.

"Shut the door!" Kenny shouted as he hopped around, trying to get his legs into his pants.

Still screaming, with panic in her bulging eyes, Denise turned around and slammed the bathroom door.

"No!" Kenny shouted, with one leg in his pants. "I mean, *get out!*"

Denise dove for the door and tried to open it. She rattled the knob, pulled on the door, but it wouldn't open.

"I *can't!*" she cried.

Still buttoning his pants, Kenny stumbled over to the door. He grabbed the knob, turned it, and pulled.

The doorknob came off in his hand.

Kenny and Denise stared silently at the doorknob for a moment, then looked at one another with wide, horrified eyes.

"Heeeellllllppp!" they screamed together as they turned and began to pound on the door with their fists.

Downstairs, the party continued loudly.

Someone threw up on the steps leading into the den, and someone else slipped on it and fell.

The girl Kenny had left waiting for him was on the sofa with her boyfriend, making up.

"Oh, Jason," she said breathily, "I never should have believed those rumors. Let's *never* fight again."

"Never, baby," he promised. "When I heard you were going off with some other guy, I got so jealous."

"What other guy?" she asked as she leaned forward and kissed him again.

Wandering through it all was Mary Hampson, drunk and still crying her eyes out, sobbing loudly as she tried to speak to people, tried to tell them something. "Yerd dum shelling yers chair."[3] But no one could understand a word she was saying.

Mike Dexter made his way out to the backyard where two pretty girls were sitting in the lighted gazebo, talking and laughing. He was depressed about the fact that his pact with Jake, Ben, and T.J. had completely fallen apart, not to mention the fact

---

[3]"Did anybody hear that? Somebody's yelling for help upstairs!"

that everyone seemed to be pissed at him for breaking up with Amanda. Mike could definitely use some
company, especially if it was pretty.

He approached them, beer in hand. "What's up?"
he asked as he went up the steps to join them in the
gazebo. The girls fell silent and turned to him. They
looked familiar: one was blond, one brunette. Mike
remembered seeing them around, and he remembered hearing that they thought he was pretty
hot . . . but he couldn't remember their names. It
didn't matter, though. He gave them his most dis-
arming smile.

The girls looked at him, but said nothing.

He walked over to where they were sitting and
crouched down beside them. "You know, I've got
some news you two might be interested in," he said.

"Really?" the blonde asked. "What's that?"

"That I recently became single," Mike said.

"And?" the brunette coaxed.

Mike shrugged and said, "Well, I remember Jeff
Gurner saying you told him I was one of the hottest
seniors in the school."

The brunette smiled and said, "Yeah, and I remember Jeff Gurner saying you told him we were
skanky."

"He told you that?"

The girls nodded.

That jerk, Mike thought. Then he said, "Well,
obviously my opinion has changed since then."

"Yeah, well," the blonde said, "so has ours."

They stood and walked past him to leave the
gazebo. On the way down the steps, the brunette

glanced over her shoulder and said, "Jeez, be a little *more* desperate, why don't you?"

"Loser," the blonde added.

Mike remained crouched beside the empty chair for a moment, then just plopped on the floor and crossed his legs Indian-style. The night wasn't getting any better.

Back in the house, the band had still not played because the members were still arguing.

"Will you take off that damn *hat?*" Walter said to Dan, the drummer. "You look like Garth Brooks in that stupid thing!"

"I do not," Dan said. "I look good. Besides, do you know how many records Garth Brooks sells?"

"And he doesn't even wear his own T-shirts," Jimmy the guitarist added.

Brian, the bass player, wearing one of the band's T-shirts, nodded.

"Okay, that's *it!*" Walter shouted furiously, throwing the microphone to the floor. "You guys are a bunch of *amateurs!* I *quit!*" He stormed off, knocking a few people aside on the way out of the room.

Dan turned to Jimmy and said, "Nice goin' man. Why didn't you just take off the stupid shirt?"

"Me?" Jimmy replied. "We were *fine* till you pulled out that stupid hat!"

"It's not stupid!" Dan snapped. "This hat is really *cool!*" He stood up and threw down his drumsticks. "You guys just have no taste!" He stalked away, following the path of the band's angry lead singer.

"Way to go, man," Brian said.

"Hey, screw you," Jimmy replied.

"Well, screw *you!*"

"No, screw *you!*"

They put down their instruments and stomped away in opposite directions.

Seconds later, Rolly Lohman ran over to the band's makeshift stage with a boom box and shouted, *"I'll* be the band!"

Rolly had been Huntington High's most serious and devoted headbanger for the last four years. Everyone suspected he would be completely deaf by the time he was twenty-five, if not brain-dead. He had long shaggy hair the color of dirt pulled back with a red bandana, wore a T-shirt that was too old to be readable, jeans full of holes, and leather bands with small chains dangling from them around each wrist and his neck. He hit a button on the boom box and went to the microphone.

Van Halen's "Panama" began to pound from the boom box, clashing with the other music already playing.

On the back patio, William Lichter was sitting on the concrete with several others. They were passing around a plastic stegosaurus that had been turned into a pipe. William was reaching for the dinosaur to take his turn when he heard "Panama" begin.

"Hey!" William shouted. "I know this song! A kid I tutored in math used to make me listen to this song! This is a *great* song!" He got to his feet and rushed into the house.

No one on the patio knew he was gone.

* * *

Inside, William spotted Rolly standing where the band was supposed to be, playing air guitar and making an ass of himself.

William grinned. It was his night. Everything was different tonight. *He* was different tonight. He wasn't William Lichter, he was *Wild Bill!* He ran over to the stage, looked around and found the microphone on the floor. He stood, held the microphone to his mouth, and made his presence known.

"Wild *Bill!*" he shouted. *"Rock and rooooollll!"*

There was a moment of feedback from the speakers. The crowd in the living room turned and laughed at the drunk, polo-shirted geek. Most of them didn't even know William's name.

William didn't care. They'd know who he was soon enough. He started to sing! " 'Jump back! What's that sound? Here she comes, full-blast and top down . . .' "

After a minute or so, people began to smile, and cheer . . . and *applaud!* William began to dance as he sang, *really* getting into the song, and before long, others were singing along. People began to come into the living room from other parts of the house to see who was singing.

"PANAMA!" everyone sang with William. "PANAMA-HAH!"

On the poolhouse roof, Geoff and Murphy sat up and listened to the sudden outburst of singing and applause coming from inside the house.

"Jeez, sounds like it's really getting out of control in there," Geoff said.

"Yeah," Murphy agreed. "You think William's all right?"

"I *hope* so. If he's not careful, he—well, God, he might never be the same again."

Murphy lay back on the roof, removed his retainer and held it up against the night sky. "You know . . . my retainer kinda looks like a Klingon warship."

Inside, the crowd was *loving* William. He was a hit!

The two girls who had burned Mike Dexter out on the gazebo earlier made their way eagerly through the crowd until they were standing just a couple feet from William.

"He's so *cute!*" the blonde cried. "Does he go to our school?"

"Of *course* he does!" the brunette replied. "I *slept* with him!"

William was lost in the song, singing and writhing and jumping.

The two girls jumped up on the small stage and flanked him, pawing him and squealing.

Vicki Compter wound her way through the crowd, both arms raised high above her head, her yearbook in one hand and a pen in the other. "Hey! Hey! Bill! Sign my yearbook! *Please,* Bill, sign my yearbook!"

Someone grabbed the yearbook from Vicki's hand.

"Hey!" Vicki shouted.

Hands began to raise and the yearbook was passed around.

"Hey!" Vicki squealed.

The yearbook moved around the room . . . and around and around the room again.

Seeing all the uplifted arms, William dove from the stage and was caught and supported by numerous hands. He was passed around by the wild crowd, still singing. By the time he was returned to the stage, a group of girls was waiting for him. They were all over him the moment he was on his feet.

The song ended and the crowd went insane, screaming and shouting and stomping and applauding. The girls on the stage wrestled William to the floor, and one girl threw herself on him, kissing him hungrily, making the cheers from the crowd grow even louder.

After pounding on the bathroom door and yelling for help until his hands were numb and his voice was hoarse, Kenny pressed his back to the door and groaned.

"Satisfied?" Denise asked. She was standing at the sink, drying off her face with a towel. When she was done, she put the towel back on its hook, then grabbed a couple tissues and wiped the rest of the brownies off her glasses. "I *told* you no one can hear us."

Kenny turned to her slowly, with a low, animal-like growl. His upper lip curled, and he looked . . . unbalanced. He went to the other side of the room, then ran for the door and slammed his shoulder against it—*hard*.

He opened his mouth in a soundless cry of pain

and slid down the door until he was lying on the floor. He rolled over to see that Denise was smiling.

"The door opens *inward,* you dork," she said.

"Woman, this is *all* your fault!" Kenny shouted hoarsely, sitting up. "Barging in here like a freaking moose and—"

"Believe me, if I'd known you'd be in here half naked and *pleasuring* yourself, I would've gone elsewhere!"

"Hey, I was gettin' my shit ready, okay?"

"Your . . . *shit?"*

"Yeah! For your information, I got a super mad honey downstairs who's waitin'—no, no—she's *dyin'* to have sex with me!"

Denise stared at him for a moment, then threw back her head and laughed loudly.

"Yeah, yeah, you go ahead and laugh."

And she did. She laughed a long time.

"Okay, fine!" Kenny said, getting to his feet. He walked across the room and sat on the edge of the bathtub. "I'm gonna stay over here. You stay over there. Till somebody comes and gets us."

But Denise only continued to laugh.

"I can't believe somebody threw it *out!"* Vicki Compter said as she rummaged through the garbage bin next to the driveway. "You don't throw away a *yearbook!* You're supposed to *cherish* it for the rest of your life!"

While searching for her yearbook, Vicki tossed cups and cans and paper plates and wads of napkins from the bin. They landed in the driveway, scattering in all directions. Tossed with them was Preston's letter to Amanda.

"*There* you are!" Vicki cried when she found her yearbook. "Oh, *look* at you! You're a *mess!*" She brushed it off with her hands as she headed back into the house.

A moment later, a couple walked hurriedly up the driveway.

"Oh, damn!" the girl hissed. "I stepped in gum! And these are new shoes!"

"Fix it inside," the guy said. "We're already *way* late."

The girl limped, trying not to mash the gum against her shoe any harder, but she stepped on Preston's letter. It stuck to her foot, and without even knowing, she carried it into the house with her.

Once inside, she stopped in the foyer and lifted her foot. "Oh, this is *disgusting,*" she said. She used the letter to wipe the gum from the sole of her shoe, then tossed it aside and hurried into the party with her boyfriend.

The front door was opened again and a couple guys rolled another keg of beer into the house. It rolled over Preston's gummy letter, which stuck to the keg. The guys rolled the keg into the living room, then made a quick turn into the dining room. At the turn, the letter flew from the keg, tumbled through the air, and landed on the floor, right in front of a guy with a broom. He was in the middle of detailing a triumphant hockey play.

"So then, see, I cut *left,*" the guy said, "decked the *crap* outta the wing, and—*boom!* Open net!"

He swung the broom; it hit the letter and sent it flying. The letter landed on the turntable of an antique Victrola phonograph with a large trumpet-like horn sticking out of the top of it. Richie was watching as Sammy used the turntable to cut and scratch.

" 'I got one turntable and a megaphone,' " Sammy sang.

As he spun the turntable, the letter shot off in another direction, and landed on the coffee table in front of the sofa—where Amanda Beckett was sitting.

Chapter 14

"**W**HAT THE HELL HAPPENED?" PRESTON ASKED himself as he sat in his car with his elbow resting on the edge of the open window at his side. The radio played low.

He was parked at the gate that led to Huntington High's football field. A few remnants of the morning's graduation ceremony remained. Programs were scattered over the grass and a fallen banner hung from one end over the arch through which the graduates had marched in pairs. They were already ghosts, relics from the past. The graduation itself was nothing more than a memory; just like Preston's chances with Amanda.

"She's not *supposed* to be with anyone else," Preston went, staring out at the field. "She's supposed to be with *me*. There was even that song on

117

the *radio!* Wasn't that a *sign?*" He frowned and shook his head. "Unless Denise was right. Maybe Barry Manilow really *did* write 'Mandy' about his dog. So, maybe I should go out and buy a dog." He laughed. "No, no, *wait.* That song *had* to be a sign! It's not like you hear 'Mandy' on the radio every *day!* I don't think I've heard it in, like, ten years . . . maybe even longer than—"

"And since today was Barry Manilow's birthday," the DJ on the radio said, "we'll be playing 'Mandy' every hour, on the hour, honoring the man who writes the songs, here on Mello One-Oh-Three."

Preston leaned forward slowly and slumped over the steering wheel. "Thank you," he said, "thank you *very* much." He banged his forehead against the steering wheel once . . . twice . . . again . . .

"And coming up," the DJ continued, "a *very* special treat. We've got the *Man*ilow himself, *live* on the phone from his sold-out show in Tokyo! He'll be spending a few minutes with Mello One-Oh-Three talking *live* to *you,* his fans! So, if you've got a question for Barry, get to the phone and call *now!*"

Preston sat up straight suddenly. "A question for Barry Manilow," he whispered urgently. He started the car and sped away, in search of a pay phone.

"Did you hurt yourself?" Denise asked. She stood facing Kenny, who remained sitting on the edge of the bathtub.

"*Damn,* woman," he said, shaking his head, "why you gotta be such a raging—"

"Oh, gee, I don't know." She leaned against the

edge of the bathroom sink and folded her arms. "I guess 'cause *you* gotta be such a self-obsessed *phony,"* she said, mocking his speech pattern.

"I ain't no *phony!"* Kenny snapped.

"Oh, my God, *listen* to you!" Denise exclaimed. "Listen to the way you talk, look at the way you *act*. I mean, hey! There's a mirror right here, Kenny," she said, gesturing toward the mirror over the sink. "You should take a look. You're *white!* I mean, I hate to be the one to tell you, but it's *true!"*

"So? What does *that* mean?" Kenny asked defensively, adjusting his wraparound sunglasses self-consciously.

Denise tilted her head back and smiled. "Ah. Okay. Fine. What*ever."* She turned to the sink and found a bowl of small, individually wrapped bars of soap. She leaned forward, elbows on the counter, and absently began stacking them. Once they were stacked, she knocked them over; then began stacking them again.

"I don't always talk that way," Kenny said quietly, without any false inflections.

"Oh," Denise said sarcastically, "then you're *okay."*

"And how 'bout *you?"* Kenny asked angrily, standing. "Miss Anti-Social, so much *better* than everybody else—"

"I *don't* think I'm better!" Denise said, turning to face him. "Anyway, why do you care what *I* think of you? You haven't spoken to me since sixth grade."

"Hey, *you* stopped speaking to *me,"* Kenny said.

Denise rolled her eyes. "Sure. Whatever you say."

"You got no—" Kenny swallowed his words, cleared his throat and began speaking normally. "You have no idea what you're talking about. That was a long time ago, Denise. You don't even *know* me anymore." He stepped in front of the mirror and tried to repair the damage done to his hair.

"Yes I do," Denise said, stepping aside to give him room. "I know exactly who you are. You're Kenny Fisher, who used to play *Miami Vice* with me in my basement; who used to sleep over at my house and needed to leave the hall light on all night; who used to buy me a card every Valentine's Day, and a bag of those chalky hearts with the little words on them."

Kenny finished fixing his hair, but kept looking into the mirror . . . just staring at himself, with Denise right behind him.

"And you're Kenny Fisher who suddenly became too cool to hang with me once we hit junior high," Denise continued, more quietly now. "Because I had glasses, because I was smart, and because I didn't look good in those skimpy little bodysuit tops all the girls were wearing." Her voice lowered even further, to a whisper. "And anyone who can ditch his best friend like that, in my opinion, is a big phony."

Kenny bowed his head for a moment, then turned and looked at Denise. She lifted her head and looked at him. The silence between them was thunderous.

"So, what?" Kenny said. "Were you, like, *saving* all that stuff up to tell me?"

Denise rolled her eyes and sighed, but didn't reply.

"Well, jeez," Kenny said, "if it'd been on your

mind for six years, you'd think you would have *said* something!"

"Oh, really?" Denise asked. "When? When you were ignoring me in the halls? When you were writing DENISE FLEMING IS A LEMMING on my locker freshman year?"

"I did *not* write DENISE FLEMING IS A LEMMING."

"Oh, sure, just like you didn't break my Cabbage Patch doll in second grade."

He smiled. "Okay, okay, but I admitted that right away."

Denise smirked. *"No.* When I picked her up and her head fell off, you started crying. Kinda tipped me off." She laughed then, remembering.

"Okay, look," Kenny said, "I told Jon Kieserman to write DENISE FLEMING IS A LEMMING on your locker, but I *swear* I felt really bad afterward!"

"Oh, that's all right," Denise said, dismissing it with a wave of her hand. "I told Diana Yellin you were a dendrophiliac."

Kenny's mouth dropped open. "A . . . a *what?* What's *that?*"

"Someone who has sex with trees," Denise said with a smirk.

"So, *that's* why she wouldn't go to the Soph Hop with me!" Kenny exclaimed with sudden realization.

There was another long silence as they stared at one another, and then they both burst into laughter.

Amanda saw the letter. She'd noticed the envelope on the coffee table, but it was only after a long period of boredom that she leaned forward to read the name written on the envelope. It was *her* name. She frowned, picked up the envelope, opened it, and removed the letter. She began reading. . . .

Geoff and Murphy were reenacting the climactic lightsaber battle between Luke Skywalker and Darth Vader from *The Empire Strikes Back* using their flashlights, along with sound effects they made with their mouths. Geoff swung his flashlight while making a humming sound. Murphy dropped his flashlight and pulled his hand up into his sleeve so it looked as if it had been severed. Then he shoved Geoff so hard that Geoff dropped his flashlight as well. Both flashlights rolled off the roof and clattered to the concrete below.

"Hey!" Geoff snapped. "Luke doesn't push Vader!"

"Well, he *should* have!" Murphy replied. "The guy just cut off his *hand!*"

They realized, quite suddenly, how dark it had become, and forgot their argument. They peered over the edge of the roof and saw their flashlights below.

"Those were our only flashlights," Geoff said quietly.

"Yeah," Murphy agreed in a near whisper. "Jeez, it's . . . pretty dark up here, isn't it?"

They looked at one another, terrified.

"Hey, man, want a brew?"

Mike Dexter nearly fell over at the sound of that

voice. He'd been sitting back, dozing a little. He'd been sitting alone in the gazebo since the two girls had walked away from him. Of course, he'd gone back for plenty of cups of beer, and they were all around him on the floor of the gazebo, empty.

"Trip McNeely?" Mike said, wondering if he was dreaming. Trip McNeely had been the coolest senior at Huntington when Mike was a junior, and there he stood, in the gazebo with Mike, wearing his frat T-shirt, smiling, and carrying a six-pack of beer. "No *way!* Trip McNeely! What're you doin' here?"

"Oh, y'know . . . stuff," Trip said, with a shrug, cool as ever. He lowered himself into the chair next to Mike, peeled a can from the six-pack, and handed it over. He pulled off a can for himself, set the rest aside, and opened it, then leaned his chair back with a sigh. "Sayin' hi to some of the gang, that kinda thing. Hey, who's the chick with the super-short hair and the tits?"

"Oh, that's Emily Greines," Mike said, popping open his beer. He took a long pull.

"No kidding?" Man, she's a little *hottie* now."

Mike grinned and punched Trip's shoulder. "Prob'ly nothin' compared to all those women at Penn State, huh? *Huh?* I bet you got yourself a *kick-ass* panty collection by now."

Trip leaned forward in his chair and turned to Mike with a frown. "Who told you I wear women's panties?" he asked defensively, and a little angrily.

"What? *No,* man! I meant, y'know, man. You're a sexual *icon,* man. Girls at Huntington *still* talk about you! At college, you must be cleaning *up!*"

"Oh, *that.*" Trip put the beer can to his mouth, leaned his head back, and drained it with a few gulps. He crushed it in his fist and tossed it aside, then opened another. "I *wish,* bro," he said. "I can't even get *digits* as a freshman."

"Shut *up,*" Mike said in quiet disbelief.

"Seriously," Trip said. "Hey, man, I thought college was gonna be the A.M.-P.M. Mini-Mart of girls. I thought I'd be writin' more true-life letters to *Penthouse* than I would term papers. Hell, that's even why I broke up with Janine before I left."

Mike turned his chair toward Trip, frowning. He didn't like what he was hearing. "So, what happened?"

"College women are totally different, bro," Trip said. He took a couple gulps of beer, then wiped his mouth with the back of his hand. "They're all . . . *serious* and shit . . . talking about world issues and economogical stuff. And they *all* wanna date older guys."

Mike's frown deepened. "Well, not *all* of them, right?"

Trip looked at Mike and shook his head, slowly and sadly. "Way it goes, man." He opened his mouth and suddenly released an earth-shattering belch. "Hell, I even tried getting Janine to take me back. Remember Janine? My old girlfriend from Huntington? But she's all cozy with some senior. He's premed. Hell, they *all* are, it seems. Guys like us, Mike—we're a dime a dozen." He finished off the beer, reached down and got another, and popped it open. "I'm tellin' ya, Mike, look out for that scrawny four-eyed kid whose ass you used to kick for fun. In three years, he'll be with your girlfriend." He took a couple gulps of his new beer. "Hey, speakin' of which—you still with that Amanda? Now *there* was a prize if I ever saw one."

Mike nodded slowly as he looked Trip over. "Uh, yeah," he said. He watched as Trip finished off his beer, and Mike realized his old idol had developed quite a gut. It spilled over the waist of his jeans and peeked out beneath the bottom of his T-shirt. *Freshman ten? Looks like fifteen to twenty.*

"You're lucky, man," Trip said. "Hold on to her. That's the best advice I can give ya, man. That, and . . . be sure to bring those rubber flip-flops for the shower."

Deep inside himself, where no one else could hear, Mike Dexter screamed.

William had learned that the blond girl was Suzie and the brunette was Monica. They seemed like very nice girls, and William came to the conclusion that they both had excellent taste . . . because they were fighting over him in the foyer. They were literally *fighting* over him! Suzie clutched his left arm, Monica clutched his right, and they pulled him in opposite directions.

"He's coming with *me!*" Suzie insisted, while Monica said, "No *way,* he asked *me* to hold his glasses case!"

"Ladies, ladies, please," William said soothingly. He wrested his arms free and put them around the girls' shoulders. "There's plenty of Bill to fill both your wallets. Now, come on." Standing between them, he took Suzie and Monica down the hall, passing Lynda Connely and Madison Sharpe, who he knew were the biggest gossips at Huntington High.

Lynda and Madison stopped and turned to watch William and the girls turn left and go through a darkened doorway.

"Did those girls just go into the makeout room with William Lichter?" Lynda asked in a breathy voice.

Madison nodded and said, "Yeah.

"They are *so* lucky."

Lynda and Madison went into the kitchen for more beer, where Earthgirl Bowman was cutting up plastic six-pack leashes with a pair of scissors.

Her real name was Eartha, but she'd been called Earthgirl by everyone ever since seventh grade, when she went off on an ecological kick that she never got off of again. And besides that, she was *earthy*. She was stocky, never wore makeup or perfume, and almost always wore denim overalls.

Earthgirl wasn't in a good mood at the moment, because she *hated* plastic six-pack leashes and the house was *full* of them. They weren't biodegradable, and they killed sea life. Six-pack leashes were one of the things she hated most in the world.

Another of the things she hated most in the world walked into the kitchen at that moment: Amanda Beckett. Earthgirl glanced at her coldly and went on cutting the leashes. Amanda was holding a dirty envelope in her hand.

"Excuse me," Amanda said, approaching Earthgirl, "but do you know who Preston Meyers is?"

"Duh," Earthgirl sneered. "He only sat right *next* to you in freshman English. But of course, you wouldn't know that." She took her anger for Amanda out on the six-pack leashes, hacking at them hard with the scissors. "I mean, why would Amanda Beckett bother to pay attention to a unique spirit like Preston? Or a unique spirit like *me,* even? Maybe 'cause she's so caught up in leading her conformist flock of sheep."

Amanda stepped back uncertainly. "Uh, well . . ."

Earthgirl tossed the half-cut leash and pair of scissors to the floor angrily, turned, and leaned over the counter. "You hear that?" she shouted into the living room. "Sheep! You're all sheep! *Baaaaa!*"

Amanda hurried out of the kitchen before Earthgirl could turn on her again. She went through the foyer, out the front door, and stood on the porch, taking a few deep breaths of the warm night air.

There was a group of partyers gathered on the front lawn, but they were quiet and sedate compared to the partyers inside. In the house, it smelled like beer and sweat and smoke. But outside, she could smell lilacs and grass—the kind on the lawn, not the kind you smoked—and a hint of barbecue left over from an earlier outdoor dinner somewhere on the street. It was a lovely night, serene and relaxing—until someone on the lawn threw up loudly.

Earthgirl had been right, and Amanda could not deny it, especially not to herself. On the night of her graduation, she didn't know half the people at the party. She might never see some of them again, and she didn't even know their *names*. All because she'd spent four years being so wrapped up in herself, in being Mike Dexter's girlfriend, in being *popular*.

And now she didn't know who Preston Meyers was. She didn't even know if he was still at the party. Amanda took the letter from the envelope and began to read it again. It was the most beautiful thing she'd ever read. The fact that it had been written for *her* made it . . . incredible.

Amanda hoped Preston was still at the party. She *had* to find him.

Chapter 15

THE LINE WAS STILL BUSY. PRESTON GROANED AS HE scooped his quarter from the change return, then dropped it back in the slot and keyed in the number again. *Still* busy!

Preston had parked by the phone booth in front of Johnnie's Broiler. The restaurant was closed, the parking lot was empty, and the windows were dark, but the large sign in front flashed brightly. The streets were deserted and silent, almost as if Preston were the last person in town. He *felt* like the last person on *earth*.

"Excuse me, are you gonna be long?"

Startled, Preston spun around and stared.

An angel was standing there, just a couple feet away from him. At least, it was a woman *dressed* as an angel. Arched, feathered wings sprouted from her back, a sparkling halo bobbed back and forth atop her blond head, she carried a white purse and wore a flowing white gown that was open in front to reveal—a gold lamé *bikini?* She was a very attractive woman with a beautiful body, but what was an angel doing in a bikini?

"Uh . . ." Preston wasn't sure what to say. He *had* to get through to Mello 103, but it wasn't every day one met up with a beautiful angel, especially in the middle of the night.

"I just need to make one call," she said.

Preston's eyes narrowed suspiciously. *What is she doing out on the street dressed as an angel in the middle of the night? And in a bikini, no less! She's attractive, but she's probably a nut.*

"Jeez," Preston said, "I already put my money in. Sorry." He turned back to the phone and finished punching in the number.

"Well, look, it's sort of an emergency," the woman said. She sounded annoyed.

"I'll only be a second."

"My car broke down and I need to call a cab, okay? I won't take long."

Preston was about to respond when he realized the line wasn't busy anymore! His eyes widened as he listened to purring sound of the phone ringing.

"Look," the woman said, "if you could just—"

Preston turned and lifted a rigid forefinger. *"Shh!"*

The angel flinched and her mouth dropped open as she stared at Preston's finger indignantly.

Someone answered the phone at the other end: "Mello One-Oh-Three."

"Mello One-Oh-Three!" Preston exclaimed, turning his back on the angel. *"Finally!* Look, I've got a question for Barry Manilow. Is it too late?"

"You're *just* in time. You'll be the last one. What's your question?"

"Okay, this is a *really* important question. In the song 'Mandy,' was he singing about—"

Click.

The connection was severed. Preston looked down to see the angel's hand on the pay phone's chrome cradle, pressing down on the lever.

"Why the hell did you do *that?"* Preston shouted, slamming the receiver back in the cradle once she'd moved her hand. He turned and stepped toward her, leaving the phone booth. "That was an important call, and I—"

She brushed by him, stepped into the phone booth, and slammed the door.

"Hey!" Preston shouted. He tried to open the door, but she flattened her wings against it as she made her call. Preston pounded on the door. "I was *talking* to somebody, dammit!" he shouted.

In less than a minute, the angel hung up, turned around, and pulled the door open. "Okay, I'm done," she said, stepping out of the booth. She walked by Preston and across the parking lot, heading for a bus stop bench on the corner.

"Are you out of your mind?" Preston asked angrily, following her. "You don't just hang up on somebody's call!"

"I think my emergency was just a *bit* larger than yours, junior."

"How do *you* know? Do you have *any* idea how

131

long it took me to—" He didn't bother finishing. *What's the point?* He could go back to the phone and call again, but even if he got through, it was too late. The guy on the phone had said Preston's call was the last he was taking, even though Preston hadn't gotten his question out. "This is great," Preston said as the angel took a seat on the bench. "Just *great!* Thank you." He walked in front of her, waving his arms angrily. "Thank you *so* much! This is now officially the absolute *worst* night of my entire life!"

"Try having forty drunk men pawing at your wings, one groom-to-be throwing up in your lap, and your car breaking down at two in the morning, and *then* you can talk to me about nights, okay?"

Preston frowned as he looked her over again. There *was* an ugly stain on her gown. "What, are you a stripper?"

"I'm a *dancer.*"

"An *angel* stripper?"

"Hey, don't look at *me.* You *guys* are the ones who come up with this stuff. *Last* night I had to be Mrs. Butterworth."

Preston's face screwed up as he cocked his head. "Who's *twisted* enough to want to see a bottle of syrup take her clothes off?"

"I don't know. Who's twisted enough to be calling Barry Manilow from a phone booth at two A.M.?"

Preston plopped down on the bench with a sigh. He leaned his head back and rubbed his eyes wearily with the heels of his hands. "You're right. I'm a total loser."

"Oh, wait," the angel said, her voice softening.

"No, no, don't say that. I'm sorry. I—God, I feel really bad now. Here." She opened her purse, dug around for a moment, and produced a quarter. "You should call him back. On me."

"No," Preston scoffed, shaking his head. "I can't, seriously. The whole thing was . . . it was stupid. Forget it."

"No, don't talk like that," she said gently. "It's *not* stupid. I know, 'cause . . . well, I . . . I've been where you are."

"What do you mean?"

She dropped the quarter back in her purse. "I was sixteen. And I had the *biggest* thing for Scott Baio."

"Oh, no, wait," Preston said with a chuckle. "You don't think I was—" He interrupted himself to turn to her and say, "Scott *Baio?*"

"I *said* I was sixteen, okay? And you have to understand this was, like, years in the running. I'm talking *Happy Days* era, *Joanie Loves Chachi."* She sat back and smiled thoughtfully. "God, I hated her. Joanie."

"You were, uh . . . quite a fan."

"Are you kidding? I was a fan club member. I mean, you don't even want to *know* about the poster collection I had up in my room. And the thing was, I always knew that *somehow* I'd meet him. Like, if I wanted it bad enough, I could make it happen."

Preston wasn't sure what to make of her, but he didn't want to mock her because she sounded serious. He didn't even want to interrupt her. He liked her voice and enjoyed listening to her.

"And it did," she went on. "Finally. Right after

his first season of *Charles In Charge,* he was doing this mall tour. And he came here. To our mall. It was like everything was finally falling into place . . . like it was *supposed* to happen. Almost like it was . . . I don't know . . ."

"Fate," Preston said quietly.

"Yeah, fate," she said, turning to him and smiling. It was a lovely smile. "So I went. And I had this red bandana for him 'cause, y'know, Chachi always wore a red bandana. I got there early and waited outside. I was the first person there when he pulled up." She tucked her lower lip between her teeth and smiled slightly, remembering. Her eyes began to sparkle. "And he got out of the car and . . . and it was like . . ." She shrugged, as if words were inadequate. "He was so beautiful, and he looked right *at* me, and I . . . I didn't know what to do. I couldn't say anything. I couldn't even move." A tear spilled down her cheek and she wiped it away with a knuckle. "I never even talked to him," she whispered. "I mean, he was right *there,* but I . . . I didn't talk to him." Sniffling, she took a tissue from her purse and dabbed at her eyes. "I think I still have that bandana."

"Hey, it's not that bad," Preston said. He reached over and patted her shoulder just once, then pulled his hand back, not wanting to seem forward. "I mean, he kinda faded from view, you know."

"Oh, I'm not crying about *him,*" she replied quickly. "Please, give me a *little* credit. It's just . . . it's been a really sucky night. Guess I needed a release, or something." She took a deep breath, adjusted her halo. "But, still, you never know. I mean, if I'd at least just said something to him . . ." Taking a compact from her purse, she fixed her makeup, sighing. "The point is, I totally realized . . . *fate*. You know? There *is* fate. But it only takes you so far. Once you're there, it's up to you to make it happen."

Preston thought about his letter to Amanda. He'd thrown it away just because he'd seen her kissing some guy. But what if that guy meant nothing to her? After all, it was a party; people made out at parties. That didn't mean she was committed to him. She'd just broken up with Mike that morning, so it was *very* unlikely she'd hooked up seriously with someone else so fast. It was just a kiss . . . but he'd thrown the letter away.

He realized suddenly that he'd made a terrible mistake, and he had to correct it. He didn't have the letter anymore, but that didn't matter. He knew it by heart, every word.

"You are so totally right," Preston said, nodding. "There *is* fate."

"I know," she said. "So, look, don't make the same mistake I did." A taxi cab pulled up to the curb and the angel stood. She faced him and gave him that big, beautiful smile. "If you really want to be with him, then get back on that phone and call Barry Manilow. You've *got* to tell him how you feel." She turned around and got into the cab.

"What?" Preston blurted, standing. He grabbed

the door of the cab before she could pull it closed. "Oh, no, wait, no, I—" He laughed. "I don't want *him!* I was just—"

"Hey, it's okay," she interrupted. "Look, you're a really good-looking guy. He'd be lucky to be with you. And I don't think it's weird. I mean, come on, I had a thing for Scott Baio, right? We *all* have our things."

Preston decided there was no point in explaining it to her. He'd never see her again anyway. "Okay," he said. "I will, then. Thanks."

"Sure. You take care of yourself. I'll see ya." She gave him a wink, then pulled the door closed.

Preston waved as the cab drove away. He didn't know her name, but in a way she really *had* been an angel. She'd helped him realize his mistake, and she'd inspired him to correct it. He jogged back to his car, started it up, and headed back to the party.

Chapter 16

MIKE DEXTER LURCHED DRUNKENLY THROUGH THE crowded living room looking for Amanda. His conversation with Trip McNeely had changed everything. That whole new level of coolness Mike had thought he'd reached by breaking up with Amanda suddenly didn't seem so cool after all. He kept imagining himself in a year with no girlfriend, McNeely's beer belly, and a pair of flip-flops for the shower.

Mike stopped and turned to a short, skinny little guy with a pencil neck. He grabbed the kid's collar and pulled him close, growling, "Have you seen Amanda Beckett?"

The skinny guy's mouth worked frantically for a moment before he finally spoke, terrified. "Uh, no?"

Sneering, Mike dropped the kid and moved on, still looking.

While Mike searched for Amanda inside, Amanda looked for Preston Meyers in the backyard, still holding the letter he'd written. She approached the group on the patio and asked them what Preston looked like.

"Preston?" said a guy holding a plastic stegosaurus. "Well, his hair's kinda . . . I dunno. Brown?"

"It's not really brown," Matt Schwartz said, speaking slowly. "It's more of a . . . well, uh . . . he's tall."

"Yeah, kinda," the stegosaurus guy agreed. "Sorta tall. And he's always wearing . . . y'know . . . T-shirts."

"Yeah, sometimes," Matt said, nodding.

Amanda sighed, frustrated. "So he's sorta tall, with . . . hair. And he wears T-shirts. Sometimes."

The guys smiled up at her and nodded.

"That's *it?*" she asked.

"Well, come *on!*" the stegosaurus guy said. "It's *Preston,* man. He's . . . well, he's *Preston.* Y'know?"

"Yeah," Matt said. "He's Preston. God, I like that guy."

"Sure," the stegosaurus guy agreed, nodding. "He's just Preston. What else can you say?"

Mary Hampson stumbled up to them and bumped into Amanda. She was crying and very drunk. She put an arm around Amanda, leaned her head on Amanda's shoulder, and sobbed, "Snow stun shy is shy sumber shess sing."[4]

---

[4] "I know who Preston Meyers is. I can give you his phone number, his address, anything."

Amanda pulled herself from Mary and walked away, knowing no more about Preston Meyers than she had five minutes earlier. As she headed into the house, she passed Sammy and Richie coming out.

"Wha' happened to Kenny, man?" Richie asked.

"Prob'ly knockin' boots someplace," Sammy replied with a shrug.

"Or else he snuck outta the party 'cause he couldn't find any shorties who'd talk to him."

They both laughed over the idea of Kenny sneaking out of the party with his Love Kit.

"Hey, look," Sammy said. He gestured toward three guys standing on the back lawn, talking. "S'more homeys come to da party!"

They were homeboys, dressed almost exactly the same as Sammy and Richie. But *unlike* Sammy and Richie, the homeboys were large and broad-shouldered . . . and they were black.

Sammy elbowed Richie in the ribs and said, "C'mon, les go blend." They walked over to the three guys.

"How's my *boys?*" Sammy said, grinning.

"Yo," Richie greeted them, holding out his hand to shake, "whassup, brother?"

The three homeboys looked at Sammy and Richie, then looked at each other. When they looked at Sammy and Richie again, their faces looked different. While they had been expressionless before, they looked angry now. *Very* angry.

"Uh," Sammy said, but that's all he had *time* to

say. The three large homeboys charged them, and Sammy and Richie ran screaming for their lives.

In the house, Mike Dexter stepped into the make-out room, still looking for Amanda. He was sure he wouldn't find her there because she couldn't *possibly* have found someone else so soon, but he'd looked everywhere else.

The makeout room was dark, lit only by a few candles that cast deep, wavering shadows. The only sounds were those of wet kissing and breathy whispers. Mike squinted his eyes as he peered into the darkness at the faceless bodies draped over a sofa, a love seat, some beanbags, and the floor. He stepped on something and someone yelped.

"Ow! Hey, watch it!"

"Shut up," Mike said automatically. He couldn't recognize anyone in the room, so he called, "Amanda? *Amanda!*"

"Shut up, dick!" a guy snapped.

"What?" Mike turned around, looking for the person who'd spoken. "Who the hell said that? I'm gonna kick your ass when I find you!" He stepped back over to the door and ran a hand over the wall beside it until he found the lightswitch.

The room flooded with light and voices rose in angry, vulgar epithets: "Hey, jerk!" "Turn off the light, dammit!" "You *pervert!*" The light revealed mussed, spiky hair, faces smeared with lipstick, and unbuttoned clothes.

Mike looked around the room, ignoring them. Amanda wasn't there. In a way, he was relieved, because if she *had* been there, Mike knew she wouldn't be playing checkers.

William Lichter was slumped on the sofa between Lynda and Madison, an arm around each of them. His face was smeared with two shades of lipstick and he wasn't wearing his glasses, so he could only squint up at Mike Dexter.

"Why don't you leave us alone!" Lynda shouted at Mike.

"Yeah," Madison added.

Everyone laughed at that and a few people made other suggestions.

"Hey, screw you *all!*" Mike shouted as he staggered out of the room.

Lynda and Madison snuggled up to William again as someone got up and turned off the light. But William was still staring at the door. Seeing Mike Dexter had made a few things fall into place in his head, and he remembered why he'd come to the party in the first place! He stood up and put on his glasses.

"Billy, where're you goin'?" Lynda whimpered.

"I just remembered somethin' I was supposed to do," he said as he hurried out of the room.

William followed Mike down the hall, through the foyer and into the living room. It had all come back to him once he saw Mike Dexter in the makeout room, acting like the obnoxious jerk he'd always been, and William was determined to carry out the plan that had brought him to the party, even though he was just a tad bit more drunk than he'd anticipated.

141

Mike staggered and shoved his way through the crowd in the living room, and William stayed a few steps behind, watching him closely. Suddenly, William realized where Mike was going. He was headed straight for Amanda Beckett on the other side of the room.

"Amanda!" Mike called. He stumbled toward her, arms open. "Oh, Amanda," he said as he embraced her.

"Mike, what are you doing?" Amanda cried, pulling away. "Get *off!*"

Several partyers turned to stare.

"What, I can't hug my girlfriend if I want?" Mike asked. His voice was thick with emotion and he looked hurt as Amanda pushed him away.

"I am *not* your girlfriend," Amanda said firmly. Everyone was staring, now, and someone turned down the music. "And you're obviously *drunk,* so—"

"No, no, wait, wait, we . . . we need to talk, Amanda." Mike tried to embrace her again but she backed away.

"About *what?*" she asked.

"Well, I . . . I've been doing some thinking . . . a *lot* of thinking, and I think"—he stepped toward her, but kept his arms down—"I think we should get back together."

Amanda looked at Mike with an overwhelming lack of expression or emotion. "Why?" she asked.

"What?"

"Why, Mike? Give me one good reason why I should—no, no. Screw that. My answer is *no.*"

Mike looked confused, as if he thought he'd misunderstood Amanda. "What . . . *no?*" he asked. "You mean, you don't want me to take you back?"

Amanda's mouth dropped open in shock and she gasped, along with several of the onlookers.

"'Cause I'm *serious,* Amanda," he went on. "You should really think about this, because I—"

"Think about *what?*" Amanda snapped. "Think about the fact that you're a childish, self-centered *asshole?*"

There were several *"ooooohs"* from the crowd, and Mike glared at the onlookers angrily.

William's mouth opened in a big, fat grin.

"Look, Mike," Amanda said quietly. "You're drunk, and we're over, okay? So why don't you just save yourself the embarrassment and walk away now."

William could see the anger in Mike's eyes and imagined what must be going through the jock's head. Mike Dexter wasn't used to being mocked. He was the mocker, not the mockee. It had to be eating him up from the inside out. William loved it. He'd come to the party with an elaborate scheme to humiliate Mike, but now Mike's ex-girlfriend was doing the job for him.

"You're the one who's gonna be embarrassed, Amanda!" Mike shouted suddenly. "You'll be *nothing* without me! As a matter of fact, you already *are* nothing! You're . . . you're . . . *used goods!* What guy's gonna wanna be with you now, huh? After you've been with me? Huh?"

All eyes turned to Amanda. Everyone waited silently for her response.

Amanda gave Mike a confident smile and said quietly, "Somebody."

"Somebody, huh?" Mike sneered. "More like *nobody!*" He grinned, proud of his snappy comeback, and turned to the crowd, raising his arms victoriously. No one applauded or cheered, though. They just stared at him. His grin melted away slowly as he realized suddenly that everyone in the room was not on his side. No one was cheering him on. No one. He turned back to Amanda.

"Gosh," she said, voice dripping with sarcasm, "you really got me there, Michael." Amanda turned and walked away, and the crowd parted to let her through.

Someone in the room giggled. It was followed by a chuckle. Then a guffaw.

Mike realized people were laughing at him. He opened his mouth to say something, but instead, he just stormed out of the room.

William was still grinning. It had been too good to be true, like something from a dream. But he still had his plan to carry out, and Geoff and Murphy were on the poolhouse roof waiting for him. He headed out of the room after Mike, hoping his buddies were okay.

" 'Whoa oh oh oh-o," Denise and Kenny sang together. "Whoa oh oh-o, whoa oh oh oh-o, the right stuff!' "

They sat on the floor with their backs to the wall,

and when they reached the end of the New Kids song, they both laughed hysterically.

"Oh, you *loooved* the New Kids on the Block," Denise said, recovering from the serious bout of laughter.

Kenny winced with embarrassment. "Oh, God," he said, "those awful acid-wash jeans . . ."

"With the built-in rips!" Denise said with a giggle. "You were a fashion victim from the womb, Kenny. A real trend zombie."

"Oh, thank you very much," Kenny said, standing. He lifted his arms over his head and stretched his stiff muscles, saying, "I'd like to think I've improved somewhat since then."

Denise started to laugh again, pointing at Kenny's huge pants. "Oh, sure," she said between laughs, "'cause you never know when you're gonna need to fit a family of five into your pants."

"Hey, shut up. These are cool."

Denise stood and looked him over. "Seriously, though? The goofy goggles. Off."

"What? These aren't *goggles,* they're *sunglasses!* Everybody's wearin' these."

She shook her head pathetically and said, "And if everybody was jumping off of cliffs?"

"Okay," he said with a sigh. He removed the wraparounds, folded them up, and put them in a pocket. "Better?"

"Definitely," she said, smiling.

"Now it's my turn." Kenny looked her over. "Those shoes."

"What's wrong with my shoes?"

Kenny wrinkled his nose. "Do they serve an orthopedic function?"

"No."

"Well, then, they really have to go."

"Oh, all right," she said, slipping out of her shoes. "And how about *your* footwear? Or is there a mission to the moon later this evening?"

Kenny relented easily this time and took off his boots. "Your feet smell," he said.

"They do *not!*" She laughed and shook her head. "Shut up."

"My turn again." He moved closer to her, reached up and gently removed her glasses. He smiled as he set her glasses next to his goggles. "Now I can see . . . your eyes."

"Kenny, I can't even tell if you *have* eyes," she said, squinting blindly. She reached out for her glasses, nearly smacking Kenny in the face.

He pulled his head back, out of the way of her hand, and grabbed her wrist. "But you really have nice eyes. You shouldn't hide them." He lifted her hand to his lips and kissed it. Then he leaned forward and kissed her on the cheek.

Denise blinked rapidly. "Whuh-what was that for?"

"Felt like it," he said with a shrug.

They looked at one another for a long moment, and suddenly, they were seeing one another a little differently.

"Felt like it, huh?" she asked quietly, leaning closer to him.

"Yep," he whispered.

Denise softly kissed Kenny on the cheek. "Felt like it," she said.

They both leaned forward at once then, and their lips met. It was a gentle, sweet kiss, at first. But as it continued, their bodies moved closer together and they embraced, held each other tightly, and as they sank together down to the ceramic tile floor of the bathroom, the kiss started to get *really* serious.

Preston drove past Molly Stinson's house for the second time that night. As he was looking for a place to park his car, Amanda Beckett was looking for *him*.

She walked into the den and searched for someone she knew, someone she could ask about Preston Meyers, but she never had a chance.

"Hey, Amanda."

She turned to see a guy smiling at her while wearing a pink bikini bra on his head.

"I saw what happened earlier," the guy said. "You know, if you're feeling lonely, you could always come over to my house later." His smile widened, showing all his teeth. "I bet I could turn that frown upside down and—"

Amanda made an *ugh* sound in her throat, turned around, and left the room in a hurry. That was the *last* thing she needed. She headed through the living room and went into the foyer, where she was approached by another guy she didn't know, the same guy she'd seen on the patio with the plastic stegosaurus. She didn't stop walking, though, hoping he would get the idea and leave her alone.

He did not. Instead, he stepped in front of her and said, "Amanda, now that Mike's completely out of the picture, y'know, I was wondering . . . well, y'know, I thought maybe you'd wanna come out to my van and—"

"Oh, *please,*" Amanda said with disgust as she spun around and headed back to the living room, where Woody Cusack hurried up to her. He'd been wandering around the party all night reminiscing with everyone about the last twelve years of school. She wasn't in the mood to reminisce about anything, but he seemed harmless enough, and reminiscences would be far more tolerable than what she'd *been* hearing from guys. She put on a smile as he approached.

"Hey, Amanda," he said pleasantly. "Remember when you let me dance with you at the Soph Hop?"

She nodded.

"Well, I never told you, but I had the *hugest* crush on you, and I just thought maybe we could finally finish things off now that you're—"

"Jesus *Christ!*" Amanda snapped, hurrying toward the back door.

Preston entered through the front door and hurried into the living room, looking for Amanda. He didn't know what he would do if she had already left. He would be leaving for the writing workshop tomorrow. He'd been looking forward to it, and there was no way he could—or would—back out now, but it was going to be awfully hard to enjoy it if he had to go knowing he'd missed out on the opportunity to confess his feelings to Amanda.

148

In the living room, he caught a glimpse of her ducking into the dining room. He pushed through the crowd after her and rounded the corner into the dining room just in time to see her going out the back door.

Preston rushed after her, stumbled down the steps outside the door and hurried across the patio. He stopped when he saw her standing alone by the pool. She wasn't doing anything: just standing there, staring at the water. He approached her from behind slowly, uncertainly at first. It occurred to him that this was probably his last chance in the world to tell her how he felt, so he picked up his pace.

"Amanda?"

She didn't turn around, didn't move at all.

Do it.

Preston moved closer and said, "Amanda, I . . . I love you." He was shocked that the words had come out of his mouth so quickly, and even more shocked when she turned around and met his eyes with hers. "I know it sounds really strange," he rushed on, "but I always thought there was this unspoken connection between us. Ever since the first time I saw you and you were holding my favorite Pop-Tart, and . . . and the truth is, I'm leaving tomorrow, so I was kind of hoping we could at least go someplace and—"

"All right, that is *enough!*" Amanda shouted. Her fists clenched angrily at her sides as she glared at Preston. "I haven't even been single for, like, five *minutes,* and for some reason, you think I'm gonna just strip off my clothes and *do* you right here on the *grass* just because you imagined we had some intimate moment that you've probably been jerking off to for the past three years?"

The chatter on the back lawn died down as everyone turned to watch Amanda and Preston.

"I mean, how sick and deluded *are* you?" she shouted at Preston. "Why can't you just leave me alone and go off and . . . and get yourself a frickin' *life?* You little shit!"

Amanda stormed off and everyone on the lawn cheered and applauded. Preston was left standing alone by the toppled lawn chair. He didn't know if he could move. He felt as if he'd been run through with a rusty sword. When he turned to leave, Preston saw that everyone was looking at him. Laughing.

Matt Schwartz walked over and patted Preston on the shoulder. "Thanks, man," he said. "That was the funniest thing I've seen all night."

Preston left the yard and headed toward his car. He was going home.

Chapter 17

WILLIAM FOUND MIKE DEXTER IN THE FANCY ROOM at the front of the house. He was leaning heavily on the mantel over the fireplace with his back to the door as William walked in.

"Hey, uh, Mike . . . man," William said hesitantly. He was trying to remember the story he'd planned to use to lure Mike outside. It was somewhere in the murky mess of his memory. "You, uh . . . you've really gotta come outside. There's . . . there's, uh—" He stopped, frozen, unable to recall; and then it hit him. "Oh, yeah, there's these two *chicks,* man, and you're not gonna believe what they're doin' to each other! I mean, not 'cause I made it up, or anything, but because it's so *unbelievable.* And they want you to come out and watch 'em, I mean, they *asked* for you."

Mike didn't move. William moved closer to him, wondering if he'd somehow passed out on his feet.

"So, uh, c'mon, Mike. Don't you wanna come out to the poolhouse? To watch the chicks? Um . . . now?"

Mike suddenly spun around and threw himself on William. He wrapped his arms around him and leaned his head on William's shoulder as he said in a quivering, emotional voice, "I'm a loser! I-I-I broke up with the hottest girl in school, m-my best friends all sold me out, and . . . and everybody thinks I'm a *jerk.*"

Stunned, William slowly reached around and patted Mike's back. "Oh, no . . . no, thass . . . thass not true."

"Yes it is," Mike insisted, shaking his head against William's shoulder. He sniffled. "They all hate me, man. And who can blame 'em?"

William was *extremely* uncomfortable, and he was still good and wasted, but he tried to make the best of the unusual circumstances. "Well, you know, Mike, they say you reap what you sow."

"Sew?" Mike said, stepping back. He wiped his nose on his sleeve and frowned. "I don't sew. Sewing's for girls. Are you callin' me a girl?"

"Uh, *no!* No, man, not at all!"

"Oh, you're right," Mike groaned, throwing himself onto the sofa. "I probably *am* a girl."

William watched as Mike buried his face in some throw pillows and sobbed a couple times. It was unbelievably pathetic. He'd never seen anything like it before in his life.

Rolly Lohman came to the doorway with a couple of other guys right behind him. "Hey," Rolly said, "somebody told us Mike Dexter was in here crying! Is it true?"

William looked down. From where they stood, Rolly and his friends couldn't see Mike over the back of the sofa.

"I always knew that guy was a jerkwad!" one of Rolly's friends said.

William realized he didn't have to go through with his plan at all. If he wanted to humiliate Mike, all he had to do was expose him. He imagined the kind of humiliation Mike would undergo if people found out he'd been crying, and for a moment, William almost started laughing. But he couldn't do it. Mike Dexter had it coming, there was no doubt about that. The bullying jock had *earned* humiliation. But at the moment, William found Mike too pathetic and vulnerable to do such a thing to him.

"No, sorry," William said to Rolly. "I haven't seen him."

"Damn," Rolly said. "I had my camera, too."

After they left, William took a seat at one end of the sofa as Mike sat up clumsily.

"Thanks, man," Mike said. "That was the nicest thing anybody's done for me all night."

"Yeah," William said with a nod, "I bet it was."

The band had not played a single number, but they were getting ready to go home. Dan the drummer started breaking down his kit as Brian unplugged his bass. Walter "The Wall" Hall started to dismantle the sound system as Jimmy went to the corner and scooped a pile of the T-shirts into his arms to carry out.

"Hey," Walter said. "Think I could get a shirt?"

Jimmy frowned. "What for?"

Walter shrugged. "For, y'know, nostalgia."

Jimmy tossed him a shirt and said, "Those were the days, huh?"

Dan and Brian nodded solemnly. There was a long, awkward silence between them as they looked at their instruments and equipment on the stage.

"Hey," Brian said. "What, uh . . . what would you guys say to a . . . a reunion?" He looked around at the others. "You know, nothing big. Maybe a few new songs. Mostly old stuff. Whadaya think?"

They all exchanged quick but serious glances.

"I could be into that," Walter said.

Dan put on his cowboy hat and smiled. "Sure, why not?"

Jimmy and Walter embraced and slapped each other hard on the back.

Brian grinned and nodded, saying, "Rock *on*."

Amanda sat alone in the gazebo, rereading the letter written to her by Preston Meyers. Apparently, Preston—whoever he was—had left the party, and the only guys left were obnoxious, drunk, sex-hungry dorks. She decided it was time to give up and go home. She left the gazebo and was crossing the back lawn when Vicki Compter ran up to her, waving her yearbook and shouting, "Amanda! Amanda! You never signed my yearbook!"

Amanda forced a smile as she took Vicki's yearbook, but it looked like nothing more than a glum twitch of her lips. She opened the yearbook to find her picture, and got an idea. When she reached her senior portrait, Amanda kept turning pages.

"Um, actually," Vicki said, "I'm really trying to get everyone to sign their *own* picture."

Amanda ran her fingers down a page and found what she was looking for: Preston Meyers's senior portrait. She read the information beneath it:

PRESTON MEYERS: aka "Pres"
ACTIVITIES: Swimming 9—12, Honor Society 9—12, French
    Club 10, Literary Journal
FUTURE PLANS: Dartmouth College
QUOTE: "Beware of all enterprises that require new clothes."
    — Thoreau

Then she looked closely at the portrait, and gasped. "Oh, my God," she said, looking closer. It was the guy she'd chewed out on the front lawn, the guy she'd said all those horrible things to, the guy who'd said he loved her. "Oh, my God!" she cried, dropping the yearbook as she ran toward the house to find him.

Vicki made a whimpering sound as she leaned down to pick up her yearbook. She was near tears when she stood and raised the yearbook over her head. "What is *wrong* with you people?" she shouted. "Don't you realize that these are *memories frozen in time?*"

No one paid any attention to her.

This has got to be the loopiest night of my life, William thought.

He'd come to the party with a plan to humiliate the biggest bully at Huntington High; had gotten sidetracked when he accidentally started to have fun; and now he was sitting on a sofa with that same bully, knocking back a brewski and chatting about Amanda Beckett as if they were old pals! It was like an episode of *The Twilight Zone.*

"You know what I say, man?" William asked. "I say, who needs her? *You* don't. There are plenty of fish in the sea, bro, plenty of fish in the sea."

"You think so?" Mike asked.

"Hey, I know so."

Mike smiled, reached over and lightly punched William's shoulder. "Know what? You're okay, Lichter."

"I never thought I'd say it, but you're not so bad yourself, Mike."

Bowing his head, Mike took a deep breath. He was becoming emotional again. "Hey, man, remember that time you had to make some boring speech and I tripped you on your way to the stage? And the whole school laughed at you?"

"Oh, yeah. I remember."

"Well, I'm sorry, man."

"Aw, don't worry about it, Mike. Ancient history." William smiled and lifted his beer. They touched their plastic cups together in a friendly toast.

"When was that, anyway?" Mike asked.

"This morning at graduation."

They both laughed as they finished their beers.

Amanda searched the entire house, but Preston was gone. She went out the front door, more than ready to go home. She looked around as she passed the front yard and went down the driveway, hoping to see him among the partyers hanging out in front of the house, but he wasn't there, either. He had left. And after the things she'd said, who could blame him? But two other guys were walking past her up the driveway, and they got the attention of everyone on the front lawn.

Someone shouted, "Sammy! Richie!" The crowd rushed toward them.

Their clothes were torn and dirty, and their bloodied faces looked like lumpy jack-o-lanterns that had been kicked through the mud.

"What happened to you two?" a guy asked.

Sammy said, "We got our asses kicked, that's what happened."

As Amanda crossed the street to her car, two police cruisers pulled up with their blue and red lights flashing and stopped in front of Molly Stinson's house. An officer got out of each car.

"This is a big one," one officer said. "Better radio for a couple units of backup."

"Yeah," agreed the other wearily. "Man, I *hate* graduation."

Amanda barely heard them. As she got into her car, she was lost in her own thoughts . . . of Preston Meyers.

Denise and Kenny stopped kissing for a moment to get their breath. They were on the floor of the upstairs bathroom, but not in the same place they'd been earlier. They'd rolled across the small room without even realizing it, and were now lying beside the bathtub, gasping.

"So, uh, lemme ask," Denise said. "You *have,* or haven't, done this before?"

"Sure, I've—" Kenny stopped himself and shook his head. "No."

"Mmm. Well, that's okay. I have." She smiled as Kenny rolled over and kissed her again.

He pulled back suddenly and bumped his head on the toilet. "You *have?*" he asked, wincing briefly at the pain.

"Have what?"

"Done this before. With who?"

"Just once," she said. "Do you really wanna know?"

He thought about it, but not for very long. He was too preoccupied with looking at her, running his eyes over her face. "Actually, no," he said, smiling. "I don't. But whoever he is, I hate him."

Denise giggled as she wrapped her arms around Kenny and kissed him again.

Soundburger was ready to play. Walter, Jimmy, Dan, and Brian were all in position.

"All right, this is it!" Walter said. "Let's do it!"

All four of them were smiling as Dan hit his drumsticks together and shouted, "One! Two! Three!" They were about to rip into their first chord, when—

Four cops burst into the room and one shouted, "Everybody *freeze!*"

The sounds of laughter and celebration that had filled the house all night long suddenly became chaotic and panicky. People began to shout things like, "Raid!" and "Cops!" and "I don't wanna die!" Flower Kowalski ran through the living room screaming, "It's the *piiigs!*"

William and Mike were in the kitchen getting more beer when the police appeared. "Oh, damn, the cops!" Mike exclaimed. He grabbed William's arm and pulled him through the dining room, saying, "C'mon, let's get outta here, bro!" They stumbled drunkenly out the back door and across the patio. Mike kept pulling William with him as he headed onto the back lawn. "We can cut into the neighbor's yard this way and—"

"No, no!" William hissed. He stopped, pulled his arm away, and beckoned Mike to follow. "This way, outta the backyard. They'll be out here any second."

They were passing the pool when Vicki Compter ran in front of them and squealed, "Bill! You never signed my yearbook!"

She'd been running around squealing at people to sign her yearbook all night, and William, for one, was sick of it. He jerked the yearbook from her hand

and threw it into the pool, then grabbed Mike's arm and hurried on.

"Hey!" Vicki cried, rushing to the side of the pool. She got down on her hands and knees and reached for the book as it bobbed on the surface. "You're all just terrible people!" she whimpered. "Awful, terrible peop—*oop!*" Vicki reached too far and fell in.

"Wait!" Mike said, pulling away from William. "The poolhouse! We can hide behind there until they're gone!" He rushed toward the poolhouse ahead of William.

"Totally!" William agreed. "Great idea! The poolhouse!" An alarm went off in William's head. *Poolhouse?* He wasn't sure why, but it made him stop and think. "Wait a second, the poolhouse. The *poolhouse!*" Geoff and Murphy were on top of the poolhouse, waiting for . . . *Mike!* "No, Mike, wait!" William shouted, running after his new buddy.

"C'mon, dude, hurry up!" Mike hissed over his shoulder as he disappeared around the corner of the poolhouse.

William ran faster to catch up with him, rounded the corner, and almost collided with Mike.

"C'mon, Mike," William whispered, "we can't stay here! We *can't!* It's a—"

Geoff and Murphy dropped from the poolhouse roof and knocked William and Mike to the ground. The four of them wrestled around briefly, but William and Mike soon fell still as the biting smell of chloroform filled the air.

"They're out," Murphy said, coughing. "Jeez, that stuff stinks."

"Okay," Geoff whispered, "let's get their clothes off and get the pictures."

They dragged the two limp figures deeper into the shadows where they wouldn't be seen if someone should walk by. Geoff pulled at the boys' clothes, posing them with their arms around one another, their lips close, a leg thrown here and there, and Murphy snapped the pictures. The Polaroid spit a developing photograph out with each flash, as if it didn't like the taste of them.

Geoff's foot kicked something on the ground and he picked it up. "Hey, look! My flashlight!" He switched it on and shined it down on the two bodies. Geoff gasped and stammered, "W-wuh-wait a m-minute, thuh-that—that's *William!*"

"Uh-oh," Murphy said, looking down at William's unconscious face in the glow of the flashlight. The Polaroid pictures slipped from his fingers and fell to the ground. "Why . . . why was he—?"

"I don't know."

"What went wrong?" Murphy hissed, clutching Geoff's shoulder. "Do you think something was *done* to him? Was he *brainwashed?*"

"I don't know," Geoff hissed.

They gawked down at their friend for a long, terrified moment, then turned to one another.

"Let's get out of here," Geoff said, and before Murphy could agree, he scrambled away, with Murphy just a step behind him. They left all their supplies behind.

More police cruisers arrived in front of the house, along with a paddy wagon. Sammy and Richie were the first ones put into the wagon, and they complained about being held down by The Man the whole way.

Partyers rushed out the back door in a flood, scattering in all directions in the backyard, some shouting, some screaming, some laughing.

Vicki Compter clutched the rounded concrete edge of the pool with one hand, holding her yearbook with the other. Spitting water and gasping for breath, she placed the yearbook on the concrete and began to pull herself out of the pool. She was on her hands and knees at the pool's edge when a wave of fleeing partyers rushed by, and knocked her back in.

"Nuh-nuh-*no!*" she sputtered, reaching for the edge of the pool again.

Someone kicked her yearbook in passing and knocked it into the middle of the pool.

"I can't even *swim!*" Vicki shouted as she pushed away from the edge of the pool to rescue her yearbook.

Cops followed the partyers out the back door, and others came around the side of the house from the front. Many of the fleeing teenagers were caught and rounded up in front of the house. A few of the stragglers were brought from their hiding places in the backyard, like Mary Hampson.

"Miss, for the last time," an officer said, "please stop crying and give me your name and address."

Her lips moved, but all that came out was wailing and blubbering.[5]

---

[5]"But I already *told* you! My name is Mary Hampson and I live at Seventeen Eighty-one Norfolk!"

"Okay," the officer said with a sigh, "we'll have to take you in."

As Mary was being led to the paddy wagon, Officer Norman Getz wandered around the corner of the poolhouse.

"Whoa-ho-*hooaah!*" he shouted. "I think you boys might wanna come see this for yourselves."

Officers Killborne and Wilder joined him and followed the beam of his flashlight. They looked down at the two half-naked guys on the ground. They were surrounded by scattered Polaroid pictures, a camera, a *Jurassic Park* Thermos with a skull and crossbones on the side, and a white cloth.

"Holy Christ," Officer Killborne said.

"Looks like some sort of twisted Satanic exhibitionist drug ritual," Officer Wilder added.

"What's that they were sniffin'?" Officer Getz asked.

Officer Killborne leaned down, lifted the cloth and sniffed it. *"Hooo!"* he hooted, dropping it to the ground again. "Some sorta homemade turpentine."

The three police officers stood together, looking down at the two boys with disgust.

"They just get sicker every year," Officer Wilder said, shaking his head.

"Yep," Officer Getz agreed. "It's that Marilyn Manson lady. Okay, load 'em into the wagon."

Chapter 18

THE UPSTAIRS BATHROOM WAS DARK EXCEPT FOR THE soft glow of Kenny's scented candle. Clothes were scattered about the room, dangling over the edge of the counter, draped over the side of the bathtub, crumpled in a corner. Packets of condoms were strewn over the floor in all directions. Denise and Kenny were lying side by side on the bathroom floor beneath a huge, plush bath towel. They had been staring up at the ceiling for several minutes, not moving, not speaking, and very carefully avoiding any physical contact beneath the towel.

Denise slowly turned her head to steal a glance at Kenny, but only for an instant. A moment later, Kenny did the same, taking a quick look at Denise, then returning his gaze to the ceiling.

"Well," Kenny said, finally breaking the silence.

"Well," Denise repeated.

Silence again; another long silence.

Finally, Denise carefully reached for her shirt, which was on the floor beside the small blue garbage can. At the same time, Kenny reached up for his shirt, which had hooked on to a towel rack when he threw it earlier. They began to dress slowly, getting out from under the towel to collect their scattered clothes. They avoided eye contact and said nothing. When they were done, they found themselves standing in the bathroom, still locked in.

Denise cleared her throat and said cautiously, "So, uh, just . . . just so you know, it's . . . it's not always, uh . . . well, I mean, it gets better."

Kenny scowled at her. "What?"

"Well, you know, like . . . next time, you won't be so, uh . . . I mean, it can go for . . . longer." She winced and covered her eyes with her hand for a moment. "Oh, God, that's *not* what I meant. I meant, you know, that since we hadn't ever done it together before, well—"

"How do you know it wasn't *your* fault?" Kenny said, sounding suddenly cool. He began to gather things back into his backpack.

Denise flinched, taken aback by his question. "Well, I . . . I, uh—"

"I mean, you said yourself you'd only done it once before," Kenny went on. "It's not like you're some expert."

"I never said I *was*. I was—look, I was just trying to be supportive here, that's all. I didn't mean to—"

"You know, 'cause my shit coulda been *slammin'* wit' someone else."

Stepping back away from him, Denise bumped into a wall. Her mouth hung open as she stared at Kenny, stunned.

"Look, baby," Kenny said, giving her a wink as he continued to pack his backpack, "it ain't *your* fault you lack da *flava."*

Denise gasped. She stepped toward him again, moved in front of him so they faced one another. "You . . . you're saying . . . that I didn't . . . I didn't turn you on?"

Tears welled suddenly in Denise's eyes as she spat, "You *pig."* She began to pace as the tears spilled down her cheeks. "I don't believe this," she said. "How *could* I—I don't *believe* this! What the hell was I *thinking?* God, I'm so *stupid."*

Kenny stopped what he was doing, his back to Denise, and listened to her chastise herself. He bowed his head in shame as she called herself stupid and told herself what a huge mistake she'd made. He turned around and reached out for her, wanting her to stop pacing. "Hey, Denise," he said softly.

"Don't you *touch* me!" she shouted. "You make me *sick*—"

The door burst open and Molly Stinson stormed into the room. Her hair was mussed and she looked furious.

"What are you two doing in here?" she shouted.

"You should fix that door," Kenny said.

"Get *out!"* Molly demanded, pointing to the open doorway.

"Don't worry," Denise said, "I am." She hurried out of the bathroom.

"No, Denise, hold up!" Kenny called. He quickly zipped up his backpack and slipped his arms through the straps.

"Get out!" Molly shouted again.

Kenny ran by Molly and followed Denise down the hall, calling her name.

"Leave me alone!" Denise barked as she disappeared down the stairs.

"Get out!" Molly shouted again, following Kenny.

Kenny stopped and turned on her. "Yo, whass your *problem?*"

"My *problem?*" she asked, planting her fists on her hips. *"My* problem?"

"Yeah." Kenny turned and hurried after Denise again.

Molly followed him angrily, staying just a couple steps behind him. "You people come in here, let my dog out, get drunk, run all over the fancy room, blast music, spill punch, break stuff, smear poop on the carpet"—she stayed on Kenny's heels as he went down the stairs—"draw nipples on my mother, throw up in my pool, sniff drugs behind the poolhouse, get me seventy-five hours of community service and a five-hundred-dollar fine, and then you break my bathroom door and have sex in there? And you wanna know *my* problem?"

At the foot of the stairs, Kenny found that Denise had already gone out the front door. He fumbled with the knob as Molly got close and shouted in his ear.

"I'll tell you what my problem is, Kenny Fisher! It's—"

Kenny opened the door and the sheepdog lumbered into the foyer, pink tongue bobbing.

"Mister Tuxford!" Molly squealed. She got down on one knee and hugged the dog.

Kenny took advantage of the distraction and ran out of the house.

"Lichter. William."

At the sound of his name, and the deafening metallic slamming sounds that followed it, William jerked awake.

There was an earthquake going on inside his head, and it was a big one. His stomach roiled and churned and every inch of his body seemed to quiver as he tried to sit up. He was on a cot in a small room with concrete walls. To his left, he saw bars, and on the other side of the bars stood a fat man in a policeman's uniform holding a clipboard.

Oh, God, William thought, *I'm in jail.*

"Let's go," the police officer said. "Time to get up." He unlocked the door of the jail cell and slid it open. "Your parents are here to take you home."

William leaned forward and held his throbbing head in both hands. "Oh, God, oh, God, I'm going to die."

"I don't think so," the officer assured him. "It's just a hangover."

"No, no, I meant—" He tried to stand, but dropped back down on the edge of the cot, dizzy and in pain. "Well, this is definitely some form of death, no doubt about that. But I was talking about my parents. God, my parents. I've ruined my life. I've ruined *their* lives." His heart started to triphammer from panic as he turned to the officer. "They must hate me. Do they hate me? Are they really angry? Did you notice my dad carrying a weapon of any sort?"

"'Fraid not, kid," the officer said, shaking his head. "They're more worried than anything else. You know, 'cause it's not your fault that, uh"—he looked down at the clipboard—"that Mike Dexter beat you up and forced you to drink alcohol until you passed out." He read it from the clipboard, but it was obvious from the sarcastic tone of his voice that he didn't buy a word of it.

"Whuh-what did you say?" William asked hoarsely.

"That's the story we got from the Dexter kid."

"He *told* you that? You mean, he said it . . . it was *his* idea that—"

"Unless you have a more unrealistic version you'd like to tell me," the officer said sardonically.

"Oh, no," William replied quickly. "No, definitely not. I was just . . . well, you know, it's just that it's so funny that he . . . um, finally admitted it. You know. That Mike," he said with a chuckle. "Always picking on me. Heh-heh-heh." It hurt to laugh, or even to chuckle a fake chuckle. William clutched his head again and groaned, "Ow, ow, ow."

"All right, whatever," the officer said with a shrug. He didn't care either way. "Just do us both a favor, kid, and don't let me see you in here again."

"Absolutely," William said, standing carefully. "I'll be sure to do that, officer. Thank you. Thank you very much." He took a couple stumbling steps and grabbed the bars to steady himself. Once outside the cell, he walked with the officer down a corridor, and stopped when his stomach did a double back flip.

The officer stopped and turned to William.

"Um . . ." William began in a weak voice.

The officer pointed ahead of them and said, "Right there, to your left."

William slapped a hand over his mouth, ran past the cop, and threw himself into the bathroom.

"That first bender's always the worst," the officer muttered, shaking his head.

Denise had stopped crying, but she hadn't stopped hurting. She made her way along the sidewalk through the dark of the morning's wee hours, going home on foot. She kept mentally kicking herself for her supidity.

At first, it all seemed so sweet . . . being locked in that bathroom with Kenny, her childhood friend. He was disgusting in his trendiness, of course, strutting around like a homeboy, using the slang, wearing the clothes. But once she got through all that, he was still Kenny, and they'd had fun in that upstairs bathroom. And then, they'd kissed, and what had happened after that *seemed* so wonderful. But she'd been wrong. She'd made a horrible mistake.

Denise heard a car approaching behind her. It slowed down as it pulled over to the curb.

"Denise!" Kenny called.

She ignored him, didn't even glance at him, just picked up her pace and kept walking.

"C'mon, Denise," Kenny said, leaning out the window as he drove along beside her in his green Range Rover. "What, are you just gonna *walk* home? In the middle of the night?"

"It's not that far," she said, walking even faster.

Kenny parked the Range Rover, jumped out and hurried after her on foot. "Denise, just—c'mon, slow down a sec, would ya? I wanna *explain!*"

"Don't bother."

He fell into step beside her. "No, no, c'mon, I . . . I'm sorry, Denise. Really. It's just that . . . in there, afterward, I . . . you know . . . I felt bad enough already, and then you went and said . . . well, how it wasn't all that good for you, so I . . . I just . . . I'm *sorry,* Denise!"

Denise stopped walking in the pool of light cast by a streetlight, but did not turn to him.

"I'm sorry, really," Kenny went on. He stepped in front of her and tried to catch her eye. "That stuff I said in there, it . . . it was really harsh. I didn't mean it, Denise. I *didn't.*"

She bowed her head and said quietly, "Yeah, I . . . I guess I shouldn't have said . . . well, you know. I'm sorry, too. I didn't mean it to sound the way it did." Denise lifted her head and met Kenny's eyes, but only for a moment. She turned away quickly, embarrassed.

"What?" Kenny asked, putting his hands on her shoulders. *"What?"*

She glanced at him again, but dipped her head. It had suddenly occurred to her *exactly* what had happened earlier, and she somehow found it very funny. She couldn't contain herself and let out a laugh. Looking at him again, she said, "Well, it's just that . . . I mean, we just . . . you and me, the two of us . . . we just . . . had *sex!*" She gasped and slapped a hand over her mouth, as if she'd just seen a train wreck.

Kenny pulled his hands away and looked a little hurt. "Yeah, yeah, we did. So?"

"But don't you think that's . . . I mean, after all these years . . . after our sleepovers and playing *Miami Vice* . . . well, don't you think that's—" She laughed again, unable to hold it in.

"Oh. Well . . ." Kenny's mouth curled up in a half smile at first, then the other side joined it. "Yeah, that's kinda . . . y'know . . . somewhat, uh . . ."

"Funny?" Denise asked, her voice quivering as she held back more laughter.

"A little, yeah," Kenny said with a chuckle.

They fell silent and stood there staring at one another.

"So," Denise said.

"Soooo," Kenny said.

First they smiled at one another, and then they burst into laughter and embraced, holding each other close there on the sidewalk as they laughed and laughed, at themselves and each other, and at the fact that they had somehow managed to find each other after knowing one another most of their lives.

* * *

Preston stared at his bedroom ceiling and told himself again, as he had so many times in the last hour, to go to sleep. But he couldn't. He was looking at the ceiling, but he all he could *see* was Amanda Beckett, as she'd looked when she told him to leave her alone and get a life.

The room was filled with packed suitcases and garment bags, all ready for his trip. He would be catching the train in the morning.

But his heart still ached from the blow he'd received from Amanda. He supposed it was for the best. He'd said his piece and gotten his reaction, and if he hadn't, he might have spent the rest of his life wondering. Now all he had to wonder about was what he had done to stir such anger in a girl who didn't even know him. But that's the way it was. And it was over. Over. Done with. And he really needed to sleep. But he couldn't.

Six miles away, in her own bed, Amanda Beckett couldn't sleep, either. She lay on her back with both hands pressing the letter to her breast, the letter written by Preston Meyers. She'd been so certain he was just another guy hitting on her that she'd just glanced at his face, and remembered it only vaguely. But his words, his feelings, they were all there in the letter, and they were *exactly* what she'd been longing to hear.

Chapter 19

JOHNNIE'S BROILER WAS A FAVORITE HANGOUT AMONG the teenagers in town, especially after a big party, because it opened at five in the morning.

Preston had awakened to a message from Denise on his answering machine: "Hey, Pres, I kinda lost you last night, huh? Maybe you're with Amanda! That would be great. But seriously, I have *got* to see you before you leave, so meet me at Johnnie's for breakfast. I have to tell you a *very* interesting story about my night."

Denise was standing in front of the restaurant when Preston drove up, and she was smiling as Preston hadn't seen her smile in a long time. He parked the car and got out as Denise hurried toward him. They ended up sitting on the hood of Preston's car as Denise told him the whole story. She told him *everything.* When she was done, she turned to him with a grin and waited for his reaction.

"Get out," Preston said, speaking quietly at first, then with more feeling. "Get *out!* You're serious? I mean, *really?* Kenny Fisher?"

Denise nodded. "Yep. It's all true."

"So, are you guys like, a . . . a *couple* now?" Preston asked.

"Whoa, whoa, not so fast there, my friend," Denise said, holding up a hand. "There's much to be dealt with before *that* could happen."

She gestured to the front windows of Johnnie's Broiler and Preston followed her gaze. Kenny sat in a front booth, right next to the window, watching them. He nodded at them and flashed a gangsta-style peace sign.

"Right there, for one," Denise said. She gave Kenny a wave, unable to hide her annoyance at his gangsta behavior.

"To say I'm shocked is an understatement," Preston said.

"Hah!" Denise laughed. "You and me both."

"Can I come to the wedding?"

"Oh, God," Denise groaned. "I really should've taken this one to my grave." She laughed, then turned fully to Preston. "Off of me, on to you. Did you finally tell Amanda Beckett how the sun rises and sets on her very being?"

Preston told her the story.

"Oh, Pres," she said, grabbing his hand, "I'm so sorry. God, that's awful. That bitch. She's such a bitch!"

"It's okay," Preston said.

"No! She's a total bitch! You know what? I'm gonna call her today and—"

"Hey, hey, slow down. I appreciate the fury, but really, it's okay. *I'm* okay. It turns out Amanda and I weren't meant to be. It sucks, but at least I finally know. And now it's over. I mean, maybe there's no such thing as fate, right? Maybe it's all bullshit. So, now I can go off and . . . meet somebody else. Somebody who really *is* right for me. And next time, I won't wait four years just to *talk* to her."

Denise laughed as Preston jumped off the hood and walked around to the driver's side door.

"On the other hand," he continued, "maybe this was all some sort of hero's trial, you know? Something to make me . . . come out a better person. 'Cause in a way, I think I maybe really learned something about myself."

Denise dropped off the hood and went to his side, giving him a look that said he was full of crap.

"Hey, look, I'm trying to make the best of it, okay?" She smiled as he got into the car. "Would've been cool to make out with her, though."

Denise laughed.

Preston looked up at her very seriously. "Would . . . would *you* make out with me, Denise?"

She smacked him on the arm and laughed, saying, "Get outta here. Just . . . call me when you get there, okay?"

"Most definitely," Preston said, starting the car. He put it in gear and said, "Peace out, G."

"Shut up!" Denise said, smiling. She leaned down

to look at him face to face. "Hey, Pres? Just judging from my little experience last night, I think there *is* such a thing as fate. It just works in a really screwed up way sometimes, y'know?"

"Yeah, I know," Preston said, nodding. "In your case especially."

Denise stuck out her tongue at Preston as he backed out of his parking space. They waved at one another as he drove away.

Denise went back into the restaurant and slid into the booth she shared with Kenny Fisher.

"Yo, baby," Kenny said.

"'Yo, baby'?" she asked. "Look, Kenny, we've gotta talk about a few things, and 'Yo, baby' is one of 'em."

As Denise and Kenny sat in their window booth, leaning toward one another over the table, William Lichter walked into the restaurant.

William's head was filled with drummers and his stomach was filled with giant wet moths, flailing their wet wings and clotting together unpleasantly. He stepped past the cashier, past the sign that said PLEASE WAIT TO BE SEATED, and searched the tables and booths for Mike Dexter. He saw a lot of other people from the party, all looking long-faced and miserable from the night's excesses. He finally spotted Mike, sitting with Jake Wickley, Ben Foss, and T.J. Munson. He hurried toward their booth.

"All I know is," Mike said wearily, "tonight I'm goin' to a bar, chicks are gonna be all over my jock, and you guys're gonna be stuck at home with your *poodles.*"

"Yeah," Jake said, looking painfully thoughtful all of a sudden, "maybe we *should* break up with 'em."

"Hey, Mike!" William said, sounding more enthusiastic than he felt and smiling even though it hurt. "I never got a chance to thank you for covering for me last night! That was so cool!" He started to sit down next to Mike. "Telling the cops that it was your—"

"Yo!" Mike shouted. "What're you *doing?*"

William froze, half sitting in the booth, his butt not quite on the cushion.

"You geek," Mike sneered. "Who the hell said you could sit with us?"

William stood and ran a hand through his hair, confused and embarrassed and *very* uncomfortable. "I just thought—"

"Shouldn't you be home playing with your computer?" Jake asked.

"Yeah, Urkel," Mike said, "go watch some *Star Trek.*"

The other guys at in the booth burst into laughter.

"Urkel!" Ben exclaimed. "That's so funny!"

William walked away from the booth slowly. He passed people who'd cheered him the night before, girls who'd pawed him and fought over him, but they only glanced at him and looked away quickly, as if they found him embarrassing.

He left the restaurant with an ache in his chest.

Amanda picked up the phone as soon as she got out of the shower. She'd looked up Preston's number in the phonebook the night before. There was only one Meyers in town, fortunately, so it had been easy. She punched in the number and waited as the phone rang.

"Hello?" It was a man, probably Preston's father.

"Hi, is Preston there?"

"No, he's not here right now."

"Oh, well, do you know when he'll be back?"

"I'm afraid he won't be back anytime soon," the man said. "He's gone for the summer. He's going to a writing workshop in Boston. His favorite writer is going to be there. Kurt Fundegate, or something like that. He's on his way to the train station now."

"The train station?" She tried to force herself to sound cheery. "Well, that's . . . great. I'm just a friend from school. I guess I forgot he was leaving. You know what? Maybe I'll just call back at the end of the summer, okay?"

Amanda hung up the phone after they exchanged good-byes. Her heart was pounding. He wasn't gone yet. He was on his way to the train station. "Where the hell is the train station?" she muttered to herself.

Someone knocked at the pane of her bedroom window. Amanda smiled as she shot to her feet, threw herself at the window and pulled the string to lift the blinds, hoping Preston had come to her before leaving town.

It was Ron, her cousin.

Her smile crumbled.

"So, uh, you didn't tell your parents about what I did last night, did you?" he called.

She jerked the string and the blinds dropped.

Chapter 20

ONCE PRESTON HAD HIS TICKET, HE WALKED OVER TO the waiting area, where rows of plastic chairs were bolted to the floor and to one another. He took a seat, put down his bag, and settled in to read some more of *Cat's Cradle*, one of his favorite Kurt Vonnegut novels. He couldn't concentrate on the book, though, so he slid it into his satchel and just sat there.

An echoing, metallic voice announced the arrivals and departures of trains over loudspeakers. The train station was enormous, with high, painted ceilings and Gothic chandeliers. It made Preston feel small and insignificant, and it reflected the way he felt inside—like he had a cavernous empty space in his very center. He felt as if something had been left unfinished, as if something was missing.

In the cab on the way to the train station, he'd told

himself that what had happened with Amanda was for the best. Even if she had reacted positively, what could he have done about it? He couldn't possibly back out of the workshop, not even for Amanda Beckett. But that *hadn't* happened, so now it was time to get on with his life. He'd go to college in the fall and meet other girls. He would meet all *kinds* of new people, and begin a whole new *life*.

"The nine thirty-five train to Boston and points between now boarding at track thirty-three," the metallic voice announced.

That was Preston's train. He stood, then leaned down pick up his bags.

"Excuse me, I think you dropped this."

Preston recognized the voice immediately and stood up so fast, he nearly lost his balance and fell over. He found himself face to face with Amanda. She had something in her hand and was holding it out to him, but Preston didn't take his eyes from hers long enough to see what it was.

"Whuh-what—what are *you* doing here?" he asked quietly.

"I talked to your dad," she said. "He told me you'd be here, so I thought I'd, uh . . . well." She shrugged and held her hand out farther.

Preston looked down at the dirty, creased envelope in her hand. Amanda's name was on the front, right where he'd written it. "That's my letter," he said, looking at her again. He was frowning, confused.

Amanda smiled. "I thought it was *my* letter," she said, taking a step closer to him.

"No, uh . . . well, *yeah*. I mean, it *is*. I just . . . I thought it was . . . gone. Of *course* it's your letter." He returned her smile, but his back stiffened when it occurred to him that if she *had* the letter—even though he had no idea how that was possible—she'd probably *read* the letter! "D-did you . . . read it?" he asked.

Amanda nodded.

"Oh, God, well, uh . . ." Preston began to fidget. "Let me just say, uh . . . I don't know what was in there because, uh, you know, I changed it so many times that I—"

"Thank you," Amanda said, still smiling. "Thank you, Preston."

Preston.

Preston was certain she could hear his heart thundering in his chest as he looked at her in disbelief. She'd read the letter, and yet, there she stood, smiling at him, even after what she'd said the night before.

"Oh, thank *you,*" Preston said, realizing immediately how stupid it sounded. "I mean, uh . . . you're welcome."

"What I said to you last night, Preston . . . I didn't realize what you were trying to say. So many guys were hitting on me because they knew I'd broken up with—"

"Hey, hey, you don't have explain that," Preston said, smiling. He tried not to show his elation, tried to hide the fact that he was *thrilled* to hear she didn't mean the things she'd said.

They smiled at one another wordlessly, awkwardly, for what seemed a long time. Preston realized his mouth was dry, his palms were sweating, and he kept gulping.

"The nine thirty-five train to Boston and points between now boarding at track thirty-three," the metallic voice announced again.

"So," Amanda said, "you're leaving now."

Preston blinked, stopped swimming in Amanda's eyes, and snapped back to reality. He checked his watch and said, "Oh, God, yeah . . . like *right* now. I can't believe this. It's . . . it's just—"

"Really bad timing?" she asked, a little sadly.

"Yeah." He sighed. "Wow. It's just that . . . I've got this summer writing workshop. Kurt Vonnegut. Major hero." He shrugged.

"That's really great. Congratulations."

"Thanks. Yeah. I . . . I can't wait." But there was no enthusiasm in his voice. All of Preston's enthusiasm was in his eyes as he looked at Amanda.

"Well, you should go, then," she said, nodding slowly. "And I guess . . . maybe it's better this way. Maybe . . . I'm *supposed* to be single for a while."

Preston tried to laugh, but it came out a dry, brittle chuckle. "Yeah."

"You know, it's like you said. This all probably happened for a reason."

"Yeah. Yeah," Preston said, looking at his feet. He met her eyes with his again and asked, "I . . . I did say that, didn't I?"

Amanda laughed as she nodded.

They stood there for a long moment, staring at one another, unsure of what to say or do next.

"So, good luck," Amanda said finally.

"Yeah. You, too." Preston didn't know how to say good-bye to her. Should he hug her? Kiss her? He wanted to both, but not for just a couple seconds, for a long time. He could bring himself to do neither and simply held out his hand to shake.

Amanda looked down at Preston's hand and frowned for just an instant, then shook.

Preston's hand was clammy from nervousness, but that didn't stop him from feeling the silkiness of her skin and silently rejoicing at the gentle squeeze she gave him as she smiled.

"I'll see ya," Amanda said.

"Okay."

Amanda turned and walked away then.

So, that's it, Preston thought. *The one thing I've wanted for four years . . . a relationship with Amanda Beckett. It's dropped right in front of me, and . . . that's it.*

He shook his head in disbelief, then turned and watched for a moment as she walked away. With a sigh, Preston picked up his bags and headed for the platform to board the train.

As he walked away from the rows of chairs, Amanda stopped and turned to watch him go. She felt sick to her stomach. After everything Preston had said to her in his letter, everything he'd wanted to say for four whole years, all the things Amanda had wanted to hear from someone, he was leaving. Just leaving.

She turned and headed for the front of the station, telling herself she had college to look forward to, and in college there would be a lot of guys, a lot of people, a whole new life. But she knew there wouldn't be a single guy like Preston Meyers, because even though they'd only had their first conversation just moments ago, she knew how he felt. She'd learned that in his letter, and she'd believed every word of it. That letter had told her everything she needed to know about Preston, and she loved every bit of it.

Amanda reached out to push the door open and leave the station when she heard a series of loud thunks right behind her. She spun around to see Preston rushing toward her, leaving his dropped bags behind.

"You know, there's *gotta* be a later train," he said.

Amanda checked her watch, then smiled at him and said, "Yeah, I think I've been single long enough."

"Perfect," Preston said. He threw his arms around her and held her close as he kissed her passionately. Amanda made a small, pleased sound in her throat as she wrapped her arms around Preston and kissed back with just as much passion.

People entering and leaving the train station had to step around them, but Preston and Amanda did not move. They just stood where they were. Kissing.

While Preston Meyers and Amanda Beckett were

getting to know one another, Geoff Piccirilli and Murphy Pelan were walking home from the party. Actually, they were not walking *directly* from the party. When the police arrived, they'd fled and hidden under a small bridge that crossed a dry creek, afraid that the police might come after them. While under the bridge, they had discussed the possibility that local police departments had been drawn into the conspiracy involving the federal government and extraterrestrials.

They felt better now, though. They had survived the dark hours of the morning and were on their way home for breakfast, having avoided any trouble with the police.

"I can't believe we jumped William," Geoff said.

"Yeah," Murphy agreed. He added, a little sadly, "*I* can't believe we didn't go into the party."

Geoff waved a hand dismissively. "It probably sucked anyway."

"Probably. All those people are *totally* boring," Murphy said, shaking his head.

"Yeah. This town is *so* lame."

"Nothing exciting *ever* happens here."

There was a sound from overhead, a low *thrum* that grew louder and louder. The boys stopped walking and looked at one another with wide, fearful eyes.

The sound grew so loud, they could *feel* it in their *bones*. Suddenly it was directly overhead.

A bluish beam of light fell on Geoff and Murphy, and they leaned their heads back slowly to look up.

They both gasped when they saw the craft, stunned by its size.

"Oh, my God!" Murphy said, shouting to be heard above the noise. "This is *it!*"

Geoff cried, "Don't let 'em anywhere near your butt!"

There was a flash of light—and they were gone.

Epilogue

Denise Fleming dumped Kenny Fisher the next day.

Denise went to NYU, where she found a whole bunch of people just like her. Incredibly bored by them all, she dropped out and started shooting covers for *Rolling Stone* magazine.

She recently directed the latest video for the Wu-Tang Clan.

Kenny Fisher went to UCLA and found a bunch of people just like him. Unable to compete, he reinvented himself as an eco-conscious vegan nudist.

He currently lives with a cult in northern California.

William Lichter went on to Harvard, where he became one of the most popular and sought-after students on campus. The following spring, he formed a software company called X-Ware. The company is now valued at over three billion dollars.

William is currently dating a supermodel.

Geoff Piccirilli and **Murphy Pelan** did not go to college. They created a comic book called *Citizen X,* about a man with no identity, no Social Security number, *nothing,* who uses his anonymity to infiltrate numerous conspiracies involving the government, aliens, and the abduction and subsequent probing of innocent people by extraterrestrials.

They are currently dating no one.

Mike Dexter went to Ithaca, where he joined a fraternity, drank too much, got fat, and lost his football scholarship.

He recently applied for a job as a mall security guard, but was turned down when some incriminating Polaroids surfaced.

Molly Stinson dropped out of college her freshman year to work as an intern for her role model, Martha Stewart. Three months later, she was hospitalized after experiencing a nervous breakdown.

She is currently working as a librarian.

Mary Hampson attended college for nearly two years, then dropped out to become a tour guide at the White House, a job she still holds. Her favorite times at work are when she is leading a group of

school children in an e.
Pledge of Allegiance or the

Amanda's cousin **Ron** is currently

Seven hours after kissing **Amanda Becket**,
ton Meyers finally got on a train to Boston. Amanda
wrote him a letter every day that he was gone.
They are still together.

About the Author

Ray Garton is the author of four other movie novelizations and several novels for young adults (some under the name Joseph Locke). He lives in northern California with his wife, Dawn, four cats, four hermit crabs, and a yardful of deer and squirrels.

@ café

Meet the staff of @café:
Natalie, Dylan, Blue, Sam, Tanya, and Jason.
They serve coffee, surf the net,
and share their deepest darkest secrets . . .

#1 Love Bytes
00445-X/$3.99

#2 I'll Have What He's Having
00446-8/$3.99

#3 Make Mine To Go
00447-6/$3.99

#4 Flavor of the Day
00448-4/$3.99

Novels by Elizabeth Craft

POCKET
BOOKS

Available from Archway Paperbacks
Published by Pocket Books

1430-02

EXTREME ZONE

Where your nightmares become reality

#1 Night Terrors
00241-4/$3.99

#5 Common Enemy
01411-0/$3.99

#2 Dark Lies
00242-2/$3.99

#6 Inhuman Fury
01412-9/$3.99

#3 Unseen Powers
00243-0/$3.99

#7 Lost Soul
01413-7/$3.99

#4 Deadly Secrets
00244-9/$3.99

#8 Dead End
01414-5/$3.99

visit the website at http://www.simonsays.com
coming soon

An Archway Paperback
Published by Pocket Books

THE HOTTEST STARS
THE BEST BIOGRAPHIES

☆ **Hanson: MMMBop to the Top** ☆
By Jill Mattthews

☆ **Hanson: The Ultimate Trivia Book!** ☆
By Matt Netter

☆ **Isaac Hanson: Totally Ike!** ☆
By Nancy Krulik

☆ **Taylor Hanson: Totally Taylor!** ☆
By Nancy Krulik

☆ **Zac Hanson: Totally Zac!** ☆
By Matt Netter

☆ **Jonathan Taylor Thomas:**
Totally JTT! ☆
By Michael-Anne Johns

☆ **Leonardo DiCaprio: A Biography** ☆
By Nancy Krulik

☆ **Will Power!**
A Biography of Will Smith ☆
By Jan Berenson

☆ **Prince William:**
The Boy Who Will Be King ☆
By Randi Reisfeld

 Available from Archway Paperbacks
Published by Pocket Books